OUT LOUD

OUT LOUD

ANTHONY VARALLO

UNIVERSITY OF PITTSBURGH PRESS

Published by the University of Pittsburgh Press, Pittsburgh, PA 15260
Copyright © 2008, Anthony Varallo
All rights reserved

Printed on acid-free paper
10 9 8 7 6 5 4 3 2 1

Library of Congress Cataloging-in-Publication Data

Varallo, Anthony, 1970-
    Out loud / Anthony Varallo.
        p.   cm.
    "Drue Heinz Literature Prize 2008."
    ISBN-13: 978-0-8229-4356-3 (acid-free paper)
    ISBN-10: 0-8229-4356-5 (acid-free paper)
    I. Title.
    PS3622.A725O98 2008
    813'.6--dc22   2008030195

For my parents

CONTENTS

OUT LOUD

IN THE AGE OF AUTOMOBILES

Cody was surprised to see Mr. Turner getting into a Toyota Tercel. He would have imagined Mr. Turner driving something more like his mother's car, a Pontiac Bonneville, or maybe even a Town Car. But of course Mr. Turner couldn't afford a Town Car on a teacher's salary. Mr. Turner wore polyester-blend dress shirts and had a habit of taking large swallows of coffee from a Colonial Williamsburg coffee mug, a souvenir from last year's disastrous field trip there. That was the day Cody had been sent home for fighting but hadn't even thrown a punch. He'd cried in front of the entire seventh grade, a humiliation he couldn't afford to think about now if he wanted to get home before his mother. Her shift at the supermarket ended at four-thirty.

Mr. Turner had already started the engine when Cody put his hand to the passenger window and knocked. A loose beard of snow fell from the window. "Mr. Turner?"

Mr. Turner rolled the window down. "Well hello, Cody," he said. He was wearing the fake fur hat everyone made fun of behind his back. "Didn't see you there for a second, then voila, there you were."

"Sorry," Cody said.

"Everything OK?"

"Uh-huh."

"Did you miss your bus?"

Cody hadn't missed his bus. He'd stayed late for band practice, then got off the activities bus when Jason Kiefer and Mike Rowe threw his snow boots out the window. "Yeah," Cody said. The boots had landed right-side up on a plow-packed snowbank. "I guess maybe I need a ride. I'm really sorry about asking. I really am."

"Don't be," Mr. Turner said. "Hop on in."

"I'm really sorry," Cody said. Again. When would he stop saying sorry so much?

"It'll warm up in here in a minute," Mr. Turner said. Inside, the car smelled faintly fusty, like a library book. The defroster sent widening half-moons of clear glass across the front windshield. "You can put that in the backseat if you want," Mr. Turner said, indicating Cody's clarinet case.

"That's OK," Cody said.

"Is that an oboe?"

"Clarinet."

"Ah," Mr. Turner said. "'The clarinet, the clarinet, goes doodle-doodle-doodle-det!'"

"Yeah," Cody said.

"Don't ask me how I remember that," Mr. Turner said.

They pulled out of the parking lot, where Cody could see the snow already beginning to adhere to the highway. The sight of that always pleased him, since he felt in some way responsible for the snow, although he knew he really wasn't. It was amazing, all the dumb things he thought he might be responsible for.

"Everyone keeps telling me I'll get used to this weather eventually," Mr. Turner said. He reached across the wheel to pull the turn signal again. A car even smaller than Mr. Turner's turned past them, an enormous Christmas tree stuffed into its hatchback. A yellow tag hung from the tree's sappy stump. Although Christmas was less than a week away, Cody's mother still hadn't gotten a tree. He would have to remind her of that.

"Who's driving who, right?" Mr. Turner said.

"Yeah." Cody tried to laugh, but nothing came out. The defroster had worked its way to the top of the window, Cody noticed. The noise of it offered comfort, the way his vaporizer did. That was a secret Cody was glad no one knew: he still slept with a vaporizer sometimes.

"I don't miss the lightning, though," Mr. Turner said. "That's one thing I can say about this weather: at least there's no lightning." Mr. Turner was from Florida. "No hurricanes either." An odd place to be from. It was embarrassing the way Mr. Turner wore leather sandals in the springtime, the way he cheered for incorrect sports teams like the Miami Dolphins, the way he pronounced lawyer as "law-yer" instead of "loi-yer," the way everyone else did. Part of any respectable Mr. Turner impression included grabbing your crotch, saying, "Who would layk a Floorida oorange?!"

"—but Delaware is as far north as I could ever live. I've got a brother back in Tampa, says he could never imagine living north of the Carolinas, but I always say to him, You know, they get snow there too. Sometimes. Not all the time, but sometimes."

Cody nodded. He tried to think of something to say about Florida, but the truth was he'd only been there once, when he was five. His memory of the place was of a crowded beach where his bucket was dragged to sea, of the strange solitary cactus plant that grew in his grandparents' stony lawn, of the alligator farm where his grandfather had encouraged him to throw a fistful of feed from a fenced-in footbridge. The feed had dispersed in the air like chimney ashes and landed on the alligators' backs, who neglected to lick it away. This depressed Cody.

"—but I've got a good little car." Mr. Turner was telling Cody about driving the car from Florida to Delaware, all in one shot. Twenty-one hours.

"Wow," Cody said.

"I tell you, by the end I was seeing phantom deer, if you know what I mean."

Cody didn't know what he meant. "I know what you mean," he said.

The snow picked up enough that Mr. Turner had to use his wipers. Cody was glad to have the wipers, since they helped cover the silence that had sprung up between them. Again. It was horrible, trying to think of things to say. How did adults always manage to think of things to say?

"I'm glad, actually, that we ran into each other today," Mr. Turner said. "I've been meaning to get back to you about your research paper."

Cody felt his face grow warm. "Sorry," he said. "I'm real sorry about that."

"No need," Mr. Turner said, then sneezed. Mr. Turner looked sort of sad when he sneezed. Cody wasn't sure whether to say bless you or not. "Have you given any thought to our agreement?"

Cody nodded. "I'm real sorry about that," he said. "I'll get it to you after the break." The paper had been about the moon, a topic of Cody's own choosing, but he'd forgotten about it until the night before it was due. The only reference books around were the paperback dictionary his mother kept in her sewing table and his father's old 1961 encyclopedia set, still smelling like aftershave, with its short but rapturous entry about the possibility of a manned moon landing. Cody had lifted most of his paper from the text—it was fun, figuring out how to reword things—using the dictionary for long, unnecessary definitions like *crater, atmosphere, gravity,* and *galaxy.* His mother typed the paper up on his father's old Royal typewriter while the two of them watched *Dallas.*

"That would be terrific," Mr. Turner said. Outside, cars were slowing to a stop. Cody watched a white station wagon pull up alongside them. "I'd be glad to read your revision." A woman sat behind the wheel. Cody stared at her, but she didn't notice him. "I'd be glad to read anything you might like to write," Mr. Turner was saying. "You've got quite a flair for words."

"Thanks," Cody said. The woman reminded him of something he hadn't thought about until now: the year before, Mr. Turner had been engaged, but his fiancé had broken it off. Everyone knew. It wasn't even a secret, really, except that Mr. Turner never said anything about it. Cody remembered the one time that the fiancé had come to school, sitting at the back of Mr. Turner's classroom reading a magazine while Mr. Turner lectured about the Marshall Plan. The fiancé was pretty, clearly ten years younger than Mr. Turner, with a habit of tapping her pen across the edge of the page, then laughing when she read something amusing. "Does anyone have any questions?" Mr. Turner had asked, and the fiancé had raised her hand. "Does everyone know that Lawrence and I are engaged?" she said. Cody had joined the others in a low, sustained oooooh until Mr. Turner waved his hands, saying, "Gentlemen, *please*, let's give it a rest." But it was too much to think about. Lawrence!

"Plus a vivid imagination," Mr. Turner said.

Cody nodded. Everyone made jokes about Mr. Turner's broken engagement, lousy puns about being turned down, turned away, turned off, and so on. Nothing too mean, by school standards. Pretty mild stuff. That was thing, Cody thought, you couldn't really like Mr. Turner, but you couldn't really hate him either. He was the kind of teacher your parents forgot to mention after parent-teacher night, drunk on Mr. Olsen's good looks or praising Ms. Trent's affability and sly English accent. You saw Mr. Turner's faculty picture in the yearbook and didn't even think of cutting it out and gluing it to a bobblehead doll, a ritual reserved for Mr. Thomlinson and Principal Wallace. You didn't think anything of Mr. Turner, really, not even the time last spring when he'd paused in the middle of his lecture and said, "Don't you think I know that everyone in this classroom is smarter than me?" His voice had sounded on the edge of tears. A U of sweat showed through his shirt. "Don't you think I'm aware of that?" Looking back, Cody realized, that must have been around the time his engagement had fallen apart. They'd done impressions of it anyway. "Don't you think I'm aware of that?" someone would say, then everyone else would break out laughing.

Mr. Turner turned the radio on. Oldies. "The only music that makes sense to me anymore," Mr. Turner laughed, as if they'd been talking about this all along. The traffic began to move again. Across the windshield, snow vanished into itself, over and over again. Cody watched, wondering if his mother would leave work early because of the weather. Sometimes her boss, Mr. Jackson, let her out early when the roads got slick. She'd show up at three-thirty with bags of day-old bread and overripe fruit, right in the middle of Cody's after-school snack, cinnamon toast with double butter. It was awful when his mother came in, ruining it, spilling bruised plums onto the kitchen linoleum and telling him to wake her for dinner; she was going to take a nap. It was embarrassing to see her winter coat, twenty years out of style, with its fake fur hood and humiliating trim, still torn from the time she'd caught it in the car door. It would be a disaster if she was home by the time Mr. Turner dropped him off. What if she was waiting on the front porch, where she sometimes let the newspapers collect for days? What if she greeted Mr. Turner in her Phillies sweatpants?

"Is that your bus?" Mr. Turner said. Cody could see the bus ahead of them, stopped at a traffic light. He felt as if someone had casually handed him a refrigerator.

"I dunno," he said.

"I think that's the activities bus," Mr. Turner said. "But I can't read the insignia."

Cody could see the back door they were biannually asked to jump from, the bus driver, Captain Leroy, shouting at them through a rolled-up *Sports Illustrated*. "You're toast, Hitchens!" he'd say when Cody lingered at the door's edge. "Toast!"

"Too short," Cody said.

Mr. Turner pulled closer. "Bluebird," he said. "I think ours are Bluebirds, aren't they?"

Cody saw the back of Mike Rowe's head, the cowlick no one had ever thought to mock, not once, not ever. Rowe's teeth wore the most awful chain of braces Cody had ever seen; these, too, were granted acceptance, as were Rowe's sometime stutter and habit of saying "templature" for "temperature."

"I dunno," Cody said.

"I'm pretty sure," Mr. Turner said. By now Mr. Turner had pulled so close that Cody could see Jason Kiefer, too, propped against his Eagles coat, its green and white logo pressed against the window. Jason had thrown the coat over Cody's head while Rowe unlaced his snow boots. Its lining smelled like frozen butter.

"Wouldn't mind having that kind of traction," Mr. Turner said. "Those tires." Cody reached for his clarinet case. If he had to, he could run. Sure, it would be awkward, explaining it later to Mr. Turner—there was no getting around that—but at least Cody had the Christmas holiday coming soon, a whole week in which he wouldn't have to see Mr. Turner at all. He'd play his new video games, watch football, slice the gift fruitcakes that always became his holiday lunches. Fruitcake was sort of OK if you smothered it with grape jelly.

"But I could live without the manual steering."

But what about the few days left before the holiday? Those would be excruciating, Mr. Turner greeting him in homeroom with a phony smile, not wanting to make him feel embarrassed. Perhaps pretending like nothing at all had happened, the worst. Perhaps asking, after everyone else had left for recess, how things were going at home?

"And the noise," Mr. Turner laughed. "Right?"

They had pulled so close it seemed to Cody they were now under the bus. The bus's bumper held a ledge of dirty snow. "Right," Cody said. The bus pulled forward, then suddenly stopped with a rocking motion. Cody felt the Tercel lurch forward. "What's the prob, buddy?" Mr. Turner said, but the problem was clear: they were inches from the bus's rear, where Jason Kiefer and Mike Rowe's gleeful faces could now be seen, laughing. Soon these faces were haloed by a half-dozen others, fingers pointing at Cody and Mr. Turner in their sad, brown car.

"It *is* one of ours," Mr. Turner said.

Cody had looked away the moment Jason's astonished eyes met his, but now he chanced another glance, and saw Rowe licking the window with his remarkably long tongue.

"Oh, boys," Mr. Turner sighed.

Jason's face, which always looked as if had just registered horrible news, contorted itself into a pained kiss—an idea the other boys quickly cribbed, puckering their lips and hugging themselves like zealous lovers.

"Comedians," Mr. Turner said.

Rowe pressed his hands and face to the glass, puffing his cheeks. This distorted his usual expression, but Cody felt he could still read its single, urgent question: should I imitate fellatio or not? Rowe's imitation was pretty good, what with the way he closed his eyes and made mmm-mmm sounds the way everyone knew adults did, but part of its power was its infrequent use, judiciously saved for ripe moments like the time Cody had accidentally worn his mother's tennis socks, or the time a bus of cheerleaders waved hello.

"Real jokesters," Mr. Turner said, but Cody detected a whiff of unease. "Aren't we lucky?" The semester before, someone had nailed Mr. Turner's roll book to a drafting table.

"Yeah," Cody said. He wished he was one of those people

who could laugh whenever. The kind of person who threw back their heads after hearing a dirty joke and said, *Good one.* But he wasn't. He was the other kind of person. He felt himself beginning to cry.

"I'll tell you something," Mr. Turner said. "Sometimes I think about all the things you kids are going through, all the teasing and peer pressure, and I just want to stop classes for a week and talk it out. Put it out there, in the open. You know?" Mr. Turner looked over at him. "What would you think about something like that?"

Cody nodded, but he was already going through his anti-crying mental exercise, envisioning a series of numbers collapsing into themselves, 1 through 10, like the ones his clock radio wore. He had failed to summon them the day at Colonial Williamsburg. "Okay," he said.

"I mean it," Mr. Turner said. "It's something I've given a lot of thought to." When Cody looked up, he saw the bus pulling away. His eyes met Rowe's, which conveyed satisfaction in these unprecedented events, already shaping themselves into legend around them. Rowe would, his smile informed Cody, never let him forget.

"I've thought about it so often my friends say they're sick of hearing about it," Mr. Turner said. "'Just do it,' they say. Have it out with them. It'll be tough, but the most important things always are. The things most worth doing—"

The problem was getting from 10 back to 1. If Cody imagined the 0 falling away, this left the 1 on the wrong side of things, requiring the 0 to acrobatically jump the 1 so that the numbers might ascend from 01 on.

"Cody? You OK over there?"

Cody gripped the clarinet case to his chest. "Sorry," he said, but the sound of his own voice only made things worse. He began to cry. He couldn't stop. When Mr. Turner pulled the car into a shopping center, he finally did.

"I was fat," Mr. Turner was saying. "Do you know that? *I* was a fat kid."

Cody, twirling a French fry in ketchup, said no, he didn't know that.

"Honestly—do you want me to tell you something honestly?—I was a fat teenager *and* a fat twenty-something, too." Mr. Turner made his eyes wide. "That's right."

They'd stopped at Howard Johnson the moment Cody told Mr. Turner he could walk home from the shopping center. It wasn't far; he'd walked it a hundred times. But not in this weather, Mr. Turner had said. Not after a day like this, no. He wouldn't think of it. They'd grab a snack, then Mr. Turner would drop Cody off at the front door. He'd even go inside with him, explain things to Cody's mother, if that was what Cody wanted. If not, fine, he could just drop him off in the driveway. That was fine, too. He wanted Cody to know that whatever he chose would be fine with him. That was an important thing to know, he said.

"Do you know what it's like being the only fat kid in a family of four boys? *Four.*" Mr. Turner held up four fingers. "One All-State track three years in a row, one the local high dive record holder, one model good-looking with a voice like Neil Diamond, and one, well," Mr. Turner raised his hands, "one kid so flabby and pale and lonely-feeling he fell asleep on the beach one day and woke up in the hospital. The *hospital.*" Mr. Turner waited until Cody had registered the necessary look of surprise. "Nearly died," Mr. Turner whispered.

"Wow," Cody said.

"Exactly."

A plate of salad greens sat between them, untouched. A fat fly toured its lone yellow raisin.

"You see? Those are things I remember about growing up. Feeling humiliated. Feeling alone. Feeling like I was somehow not allowed into everyone else's happiness. That's a state crime, by the way, in Florida. Not feeling tan and happy." His look told Cody that this was a kind of joke.

Cody attempted a laugh. "Not feeling tan," he said.

"In grade school they called me Lardwrence. 'Lardwrence, how did you get to be so fat?' or 'Hey, Lardwrence, what's shakin' —besides you?' Go ahead, laugh. Some of it seems funny now, doesn't it?"

Cody shook his head.

"Well, you better believe I laughed it off. What else could I do?" Mr. Turner forked a lettuce leaf without bringing it to his lips. "I imagine you know a little bit about that."

Cody tugged at his coat sleeve. The one he'd used to wipe his stupid tears away. "I dunno." That's what he'd been, stupid; stupid to let the incident get to him; stupid to ask Mr. Turner for a ride in the first place; stupid to cry in front of his teacher, stupid to accept Mr. Turner's offer of a quick meal.

"That's something we have in common, isn't it?"

Cody nodded, a gesture that felt required of him.

"I've seen the way they tease you," Mr. Turner said. "Did you know that?" He took a bite of lettuce. "I've seen it for a long time now."

Cody shrugged. "It's not so bad."

"No, Cody." Mr. Turner shook his head. "Do you know what that is? Do you know what you just had?"

Before Cody could answer, Mr. Turner said, "A Junk Thought, that's what. Do you know what a Junk Thought is? It's all those thoughts in your head that keep telling you things are OK when things are definitely not OK. Because accepting things the way they are is hard to do. Really hard. But worth it, Cody, so, so *worth it*." He gave Cody a look above the rims of his glasses. "Trust me. It took me most of my life to figure this out. A long, long time. My life was a series of Junk Thoughts. Had them every day. It was like I woke up in the morning feeling lousy about myself, spent most of the day feeling worse, went to bed feeling even worse than when I started. You see what I mean? Just like they say; it's a cycle. Right? It's like—" Mr. Turner described a circle in the air. "You know? Like, 'Help! I'm trapped! Who can help me? I'm all alone!'"

"Right."

"Well, you're *not* all alone," Mr. Turner said, as if Cody had been arguing this. "No one is. That's something Justine helped me to see. Justine helped me come to terms with my Junk Thoughts." Mr. Turner nodded. "That's something I'll always owe Justine."

"That was nice of her," Cody said.

Mr. Turner went on as if he hadn't heard. "Do you know that Justine was the first woman I was ever seriously involved with? I mean seriously involved with. In a mature, adult relationship. I never even went to my senior prom. I never really even went on a date until my senior year of college. That's the truth. Do you know how old I was the first time I ever even kissed a girl?"

"Well—"

"Twenty-*two*!" Mr. Turner said. "Twenty-two years old and kissing a girl for the first time." Mr. Turner clicked his tongue. "Tough to think about."

The waitress brought them the bill, which Mr. Turner tucked beneath his placemat. "In college I was always hitting the library when my friends were hitting the bars. Most of them were in fraternities, partying it up, having a social life I could only dream about as I sat in the reading room and wished I was anywhere else." He shook his head, ruefully. "Justine always said she couldn't believe I'd spent my time that way. She was the complete opposite, of course. Studious, but fun."

Cody understood that it was his job to nod.

"Oh, she knew how to have fun."

Outside, the snow had stopped, but it looked deeper than Cody had realized. If it snowed tonight, maybe they wouldn't have school tomorrow. A blizzard and Cody might not have to return until after the holiday.

"People say, 'Sorry to hear about you and Justine,' or 'We're sorry to hear things didn't work out,' and I always say 'Why? There's nothing sorry about it.' Am I sorry we're not together right now? Well, yes, I am. I admit that. I'd be lying if I said otherwise. But the fact is, Justine was the greatest thing that ever happened to me. Ever. And there's just no way I can look back at having that kind of experience as—" he held his hands apart, "as, as anything to be sorry for." Cody chanced a look; he saw that Mr. Turner had his eyes closed. When Mr. Turner spoke next it was in a whisper. "Do you know why I'll get over Justine?"

Cody didn't say anything.

"Because I've got *self-respect*," Mr. Turner said, and brought his hands to his face. He made tiny whimpering noises. His shoulders shook. "That's what I've got."

Cody watched, imagining Mr. Turner telling his mother all about missing the bus, about the taunting. He imagined Mr. Turner telling her all about Justine. He imagined him saying he loved her. It was the idea of Mr. Turner sitting at their kitchen table, whose fourth leg sometimes fell off for no reason whatsoever, that informed Cody he had to decide something. That was certain. He would have to make a choice. But it wasn't until Mr. Turner announced he'd left his wallet in the Tercel that the decision revealed something of itself to Cody. Mr. Turner said, "I'll be back in a second," and stood from the table. "You hold the fort, OK?" Mr. Turner donned his furry hat and pushed through the heavy glass doors to the parking lot.

It was cold outside; the wind was up. When Cody pushed through the side door, he found himself in the hotel parking lot. It was the lot he sometimes cut across coming home from Walgreens, his pockets stuffed with trading cards. The lot was bordered by a stand of pine trees, whose boughs hid the entrance to a dirt path that led to Cody's neighborhood. The sight of virgin snow there pleased Cody, as did the view the path eventually afforded him: the front lot, Mr. Turner riffling through the Tercel, searching for his lost wallet. For a moment Cody wondered if he should call out to him. Should he? Should he let him know he was heading home? Should he say thanks for the ride? Didn't he owe that to Mr. Turner? He couldn't decide. And that was the thing: even as Cody entered his neighborhood, even as he shook snow from the heels of his boots, even as he opened his front door, he felt like he was still deciding.

THE WALKERS

The couple with the baby stroller walks the neighborhood at four. They make an athletic-looking pair, she in gray sweatpants, a yellow Walkman strapped to her arm, he with a striped headband and a V of sweat showing through his T-shirt, although it is not especially hot outside. Has he just come from a tennis match or the treadmill? They are the kind of people that would own a treadmill. The treadmill looking out onto a lawn that slopes toward the manmade pond we have only ever seen the station wagon couple attempt to fish, both clearly in retirement, the husband toting an ancient creel and robot-walking the water's edge in hip-waders meant, we assume, for river fishing. The wife does not fish. She stays in the station wagon, smoking, reading *TV Guide*. That is what we love about this wife, her indifference to her husband's curses, his line snagged in the poplars that have always struck us as looking a little out of place, like dinner candles stuck into a cupcake. Whose idea were these? Anyway, we'd love for them to say hello sometime. But we understand if they prefer to keep to themselves. That's something we understand, completely. We're not trying to change that.

Already we've forgotten about the baby stroller couple. Our forgetting reminds us that although we are interested in these couples, these walkers, that we in some way feel ourselves to be connected to them, we do not actually know them. Their daily passing both draws us closer and pushes us back like a poorly planned series of chess moves. We want to know them, but how? How much we would like to say, "Oh, I saw the Mosers today, pushing little Gregory in his stroller. You wouldn't believe his grip! Patty says he's almost sleeping through the night now, but Brad made a face like, *Oh, don't you believe it*, when Patty was fixing Gregory's hat. They said we should stop by sometime." What would they say if we stopped to ask about the baby? Surely people stop and ask about the baby. We could be people like that. *Well, they seem nice*, the stroller couple would think, watching us walk away. *I wonder which house is theirs.*

We would like to know these walkers, so we walk. *Look, we're walkers, too*, our walks say, although when we come across other walkers, we become suddenly shy. We give the walkers one look, a quick glance, trying to determine if they're in a saying hello sort of mood. Not everyone is, of course. This is not a problem. It is completely fine for them to walk their own walk, thinking their own walking thoughts, all those hopes and worries and even nothing-at-all thoughts like *Should we have asparagus or salad?* visiting them as often as they visit us, these two walkers they see glancing up, then immediately away, as if we've spotted a rare bird. It is absolutely OK to ignore us, because we, if the walkers should ever stop to ask—and we're not saying that this is a prerequisite to gaining our good graces—

are absolutely respectful of privacy and quiet. We really are. We spend entire Sundays silently reading the *Times*, sipping coffee and sock-footing it around the living room, like visitors to a shrine. Even the radio, that favorite drone, is asked to hold it in for another day. If the walkers would ever care to stop, they might find that we, lovers of music and sunflowers and quiet neighborhoods like this, this wonderful wooded loop, so horribly, embarrassingly named Beaver Circle!—how could they not find this funny as we do, yet another bond!—we, too, love quiet and privacy. That is the purpose of a neighborhood like ours, isn't it? Privacy. Solitude. To look out one's window and feel no one looking in. To lock one's door at night with a certain satisfaction, like closing the heavy-lidded eye of some fantastic dragon. But we're being absurd. We are nothing like a dragon. We subscribe to *Newsweek*. We know you do, too. But what's with *Teen People*? Just curious.

The man with the three-legged dog walks around five-thirty. Seven in the summertime. We've wondered about him. We've had conversations about him, usually during our own walk, whose time we change solely for the purpose of bumping into as many other walkers as possible. "What's with the man with the three-legged dog?" we've said. We've gotten several hellos from the three-legged dog man, even an enthusiastic lick from the three-legged dog, whose walk, now that we're on the subject, is surprisingly agile, elegant almost, like a dancer who's lost a shoe, but not the downbeat. He (we've been too shy to ask its name) has a remarkably long tongue, a sweet disposition, too. His owner follows him with an empty bread bag in one hand, a rolled-up newspaper in the other. This fastidiousness leads us to think that these are city people, this man and dog, more accustomed to heavily trafficked parks with only a few slim rectangles of grass for relief. The man has sometimes worn a leather coat and rimless glasses, furthering our suspicion. Not that we're suspicious. We love the city. We love the whiff of fine dining, missed buses, and bowed cellos these walkers bring.

We have a story about the three-legged dog man. It goes something like this: the three-legged dog man moved from the city with his three-legged dog and a beautiful woman. Why shouldn't she be beautiful? They'd lived in an apartment overlooking a park, where they walked together, the dog on a short leash, leaves crunching underfoot, the dog drawing attention, children's hands, sympathy, questions, consolations. The dog circling the pretzel vendor, chasing stray napkins, testing the waters of the duck pond, where bread crumbs float. Their walks somehow amplifying the city around them, saying *Yes!* to skyscrapers, streetlights, benches, the homeless. How could the move to this small, suburban neighborhood, with only a trace of hustle and let's just forget bustle, not disappoint the woman? This little neighborhood of gardeners and walkers closing in on her like a pulled belt. Not *another* kiddie pool. Enough already with the garden trolls. Why no public transportation to the farmer's market?

She left him. He pleaded for her to stay. He gave reasons. She gave hers. They drove to the little bus station on the edge of town, the one that has always seemed so sad to us, with all those travelers just passing through, toting duffel bags the size of trash cans, who will never know the pleasure of a walk like ours, and parted. The dog licked her hand. The bus was late and gave off the smell of old fruit. The man helped her with her bags. She took a seat in front. They kissed. When the bus pulled away, we like to imagine the dog howling. Why not? This, the image the man cannot shake, even when we rub our hands through the dog's fur: the bus pulling out of the station, the dog straining against his leash. Is it any wonder he's forgotten to ask our names? That's the thing we would say, if he ever chose to apologize for not introducing himself sooner. Don't worry about it, we'd say. Please.

But is it our fault that we cannot remember the name of the woman who walks with a stick? Yes, she introduced herself once, when we were admiring her bird feeders, but no, we did not hear, and no, were not about to ask again. Helen, Ellen, or Eleanor? Anyway, amazing bird feeders. One shaped like a sundial, another a vertically hung hotel, with dozens of perches shooting out from apertures in the long feed column. Could a whole flock feed at once? we wanted to ask, but didn't. Honestly, we love birds, but keep forgetting to fill the one feeder we have, the one we picked up at a craft fair for what seemed like a song, but maybe wasn't after all. We've never seen a single bird under its hand-painted roof, although every squirrel in town seems to know its address. They keep showing up, performing their little squirrel acrobatics along the branch we thought would be skinny enough to discourage them, but has only seemed to embolden them, the way they flip onto the feeder's roof, then swing underneath all in one motion. That's the thing we would like to ask the stick woman: how do you keep the squirrels away?

Maybe this explains the stick, which looks too long for her, we think. A squirrel baton. Sometimes we've seen the stick woman carrying the stick like a tied fishing pole, the stick's tip nearly dragging the ground, the woman glancing at us with a look we can only describe as grandmotherly. Really, the stick doesn't match her at all. The stick is thick at one end, tapering to a crooked point. Whatever bark once enshrouded this stick has since been stripped, calling to mind exposed bone. Which is why we would ask the stick woman why she bothers to carry the stick at all, if her walk ever took her to our front door, where we, feigning surprise, would just be closing it behind us, getting ready for a nice evening walk. Oh, hello. Nice evening, yes. The stick woman would describe semicircles in the lawn, perhaps wanting to explain herself, perhaps wanting to be invited in, but shy. Like *us*! There's no end to what we might have in common.

Lovely yard, she'd say. We imagine her talking this way.

Thanks, we'd say. Horrible, awkward, fellowship-draining silence. The stick woman looking away.

Would you mind if we asked you to look at something?

The side yard would be damp, as it always seems to be.

Our feet would make tiny sucking sounds, the stick woman sticking her stick into the ground. The stick woman—in our yard! We'd show her our bird feeder, explain the problem.

I see, she'd say.

We've never had a single bird, we'd confess. Not one.

I see, she'd say, then lift her stick toward the feeder. Up close, the stick woman would be much prettier than we'd imagined. Whatever history we'll make for her will have to make allowances for her former beauty, enduring into the present like a smooth stone. We'll have to explain, too, her surprising strength, this woman in support shoes who still manages to unhook our squirrel feeder and carry it across the yard on the end of her stick, that suddenly purposeful, suddenly apt stick. She'll raise the feeder to the lone tree in our front yard, the one we've always thought looked like a broccoli spear, and hook it to a tall, leafy branch.

Birds won't go to shadow, she'll explain.

As if on cue, birds will descend upon the feeder, although we haven't filled it in months. Cardinals, robins, and nuthatches. Blue jays, even. These birds will feast upon old husks collecting in the corners of the feeder like hard dust.

Sometimes they need a little shine, stick woman will say.

Walkers, this is how we imagine you: magicians, soothsayers, worldly and wise. People we wish not only to know, but perhaps to become a little bit like, too, if our saying so doesn't frighten you. We don't want to frighten you. Please know that we regret thinking of you as stick woman, couple with the stroller, three-legged dog man, and so on. These names reduce you, the you we so earnestly wish to know better. We know that you are like us, with full, complex, mysterious lives not fully knowable to anyone else, if even known to yourselves. But we do not wish to philosophize. We wish to say, "Hi Steven, did your mother enjoy her visit? Was that Becky's clarinet case we saw lying on the storm drain? We put it on your porch, just to be on the safe side. No problem. We know you'd do the same for us." Love and community. Fellowship and mystery. What's wrong with a little philosophy?

The bare-chested jogger jogs around six. He wears black jogging shorts with three thick stripes down the side. His shoes, taken into the future, would arouse wonder and speculation; they do so already, composed, as they seem to be, out of whale hide, airplane parts, synthetic rope, and the stomachs of tennis balls. Passing, they make a noise like stripping pillows. This is how we experience you, jogger: a sudden, surprising breath in our ear, intimate as a lover's; a face flushed with exertion, eyes looking away; a pink, fleshy back glistening with sweat, revealing a small constellation of moles we've wondered if you should have a doctor examine. Despite his bare torso, the jogger wears a silver watch, which can't be a good choice, we think. All that moisture. All that sun. The jogger jogs at twice our speed, passing us by. What does the neighborhood look like at double speed?

It's a good run, he would say, if we ever had the courage to address him. Plenty of flat stretches, lots of shade. Not too many cars.

But have you noticed the house with the white piano? we'd say. You have to look through the gap in the hedges to see it.

Yes, I've noticed it. Sometimes I've even imagined myself playing it.

Oh, so have we! So have we!

And sometimes I use the house with the white piano as a half-mile marker.

Really?

Yes.

Because sometimes we use the house with the white piano as a way of settling disputes. Like, we'll say, If the white piano has its lid up, that means we should spend Thanksgiving back east. Down, we head south.

Interesting.

We have so much in common! You must have noticed the woodpile that looks like a skull chewing on hot dogs, then.

Hot dogs? I've always thought they looked more like cigars.

Cigars, of course!

My favorite is the house with two hammocks, though. I've invented a whole history of the family, whom I imagine to be in the shipbuilding business. Sometimes I wave to the youngest when he's out kicking a football over the gazebo.

The gazebo! We've always hoped to seek shelter there during a rainstorm, but have never really had the chance.

Oh, it's nice all right. Smells a little like wood chips inside.

You've been?

Just for a second, when no one was around. The roof is painted silver underneath.

Silver!

But I usually stick to the road. Got to keep the heart rate up, you know?

Right.

And, like that, the tide of our friendship ebbs away. Not that we're suggesting anyone is to blame, or let us down, or left us behind. Not at all. We do not imagine that our walks grant us free membership to the private lives of those around us, as we've already said, but, really, isn't that the way it should be? Isn't our silence, our averted glances, a sign of some spiritual crimp? We are, after all, social creatures. We love the sun filtering in through the trees, as you do; love spotting a red-headed woodpecker taking flight; greet the mailman's daily arrival with an almost childish glee. Which reminds us: why must he listen to his headphones at such a high volume? We have no problem with the radio, surely the job must get dull, we understand. But why can't we shake the feeling that he's somehow trying to drown us out, us pretending we just happened to open the door when he reaches the front porch, his black boots thunking the wood steps we've repainted twice now, although he never seems to have noticed? We offer him our most sincere thanks, and take the mail from his hands without even so much as a smile or a you're welcome or a no problem or any of those responses which really mean the world when you stop to think about it. He turns, clunks down the steps, crosses our front lawn without even touching the flagstone walkway we designed with him in mind. He hefts his bag across his shoulder, grunts. Crossing our driveway, he kicks a small stone, which dings off our garbage cans. Not that we mind. Is this the wage of a paid walk? we wonder. Is there no pleasure in it?

Pleasure? we imagine him saying, the day he accepts a glass of our fresh-brewed iced tea. It's my *job*.

Yes, we know, we'd say. But it's still a nice walk.

Here, he says, try this for size. He puts the bag across our shoulder. A feeling like pushing a car from a snowbank. My God! we say. How do you manage! This pleases him.

Heavy, eh? he says. You should try it in the rain. He takes a sip of tea, surprisingly daintily for a man with D E V I L painted across his fingernails. He smacks his lips. This tea is fucking delicious, he says.

We tell him thanks. We like this mailman. We like his hat. Tell us, we say, do you ever take a few free samples? Detergent and shampoo, whatever. We won't tell, we say.

He turns a look on us like we've asked his mother's hand in marriage. Never, he says. That's a first-class ticket to the unemployment office. That's a federal crime, what you're saying.

We had no idea, we say.

You gotta keep on your toes, he says. No freebies, no special favors, no rides, no nothing.

We see, we say. But isn't it nice getting outside when everyone else is stuck inside an office?

He considers this. Chews an enormous ice cube, spits it out. A morning route is okay, he admits. I used to have a morning route. Saw a red fox chasing a wild turkey once.

We love the sound of that, *a morning route*. We've taken

several morning routes, especially in summer, when it's already hot by nine. The morning route brings morning walkers, like the two women who might be sisters, mother and daughter, or aging lesbians. Or all three! we've joked. But we do not mean to joke. We wish to know these two, who both seem overdressed for the occasion, always in peasant skirts and cotton blouses. The women are in their late fifties, or early sixties, or older. Like everything else about them, we simply do not know. It is nearly impossible to tell which one is older, for on some days the woman we always thought was the mother appears much younger to us, flipping the other woman to the mother's spot, and vice versa, like two children on a teeter-totter. We imagine the two women to be friends with stick woman, although we've never actually seen them out walking together. But we can imagine this, and have sometimes wondered if the three of them constitute a coven of benign witches, which wouldn't surprise us in the least. It really wouldn't. We can envision the three of them gathered around a fire—there is a charred-looking leaf barrel in stick woman's yard—talking in witch talk, which we imagine to be kind, lighthearted, punctuated by arm taps and silent fits of laughter. They joke. They console. They do not chant.

Good morning, they say, although it is a bit drizzly. A single curl of smoke rises from the leaf barrel.

Good morning, we say.

My, the mother says, you two certainly do a bit of walking. Laughs.

We see you all the time, the daughter says.

Really?

Mmm, stick woman says. She stirs the barrel with her stick, summoning a flicker of sparks from its interior. The smoke gives off an odor of damp leaves.

We like to walk, we say.

We know! they laugh—not cackle. Around the barrel, sacks of leaves slump like tossed dough. Sticks crisscrossed into rectangles.

We've been watching you, stick woman says.

For a while, the mother says. She breaks a stick in two, drops it into the barrel.

The daughter takes a fistful of leaves and shakes them, one at a time, into the barrel. Her hands wear a ring on each finger. We even have a name for you two, she says.

Oh, don't tell them! the mother says.

The daughter puts a hand to her mouth. They won't mind, she says.

We won't mind, we say. Already we feel ourselves on the brink of membership, wonderful, blissful membership, at long last. The feeling of wiping our feet on a welcome mat while handing over a bottle of ribbon-tied wine.

The Walkers! the daughter says, then bursts into laughter.

The Walkers! the mother says.

That's what everyone calls you, stick woman explains.

The Walkers?

The women nod. A tiny flame licks the barrel's lip, then disappears.

For how long?

Since, oh, I don't know how long, stick woman says.

Since forever, the daughter says. She gives us a look, waiting, we suppose, for us to laugh, too. When we walk away, we can hear them, the three of them, whispering. Our pace quickens. We feel our faces grow warm.

The Walkers. Terrible name! So undeserved, we think. So clearly another way of saying The Outsiders, The Unknowns, The Nobodies, The No Ones, The Whatevers, The Marginalized, The Wanderers, The Dispossessed, The Broken-Downs, The Aimless, The Forgottens, The Forgettables, The No Names, The Whoevers—The Lonely. Lonely? Neighbors, haven't all of our walks been a sign of our loneliness, both yours and ours? Why else would we walk? For what walker could not imagine the possibility of finding another walker even as they button their windbreaker and double-tie their shoes? We walk upon the claws of loneliness itself, forcing its paws back into the cage. We snuff it out with every step, like crushing a thousand carelessly dropped matches. We walk to aid you in your loneliness, and you in ours. This, it seems to us, the heart of the matter.

But how quickly our anger passes. We are fickle. We are afraid of the dark, still. How we hate locking the doors and latching the windows, whose panes show us back to ourselves, wishing the night to pass, so that another day, with its promise of walks, might swing around again. We think of you, thinking, perhaps, of us. This thought pleases us. Because we have always thought ourselves to be a little bit like you, and because you have taken up such a good portion of our thoughts. Not that we mind. We weren't suggesting that we mind. The thought of you sustains us, and lends meaning to our walks. Is this the same for you? We leave a porch light on, as a sign of our hope and regret. Also, because we've been hearing some scratching noises out there lately. Probably nothing. Cats or squirrels. Raccoons, maybe.

—

Visitors arrive. Old friends from the city. Their visit draws us out of the neighborhood and into downtown, to the one restaurant that serves Pellegrino, to the art theater where one of our old, donated couches still serves as seating, to the city park, where the walkways seem less interesting to us now, despite the new brickwork paths that lead walkers to a half-circle of sitting benches and a new goldfish pond, the goldfish as large as footballs. We drop breadcrumbs and talk about the city. Yes, we sometimes miss it. No, we haven't been back in a while. Yes, we would love some good Thai. Yes, we would love to go to the theater. No, we weren't kidding: the only taxi in town is an El Camino.

Our friends shake their heads, say My God. We couldn't imagine.

But we love it here, we say. We really do.

Our friends say, What do you love best about it?

It is late when we arrive back in the neighborhood, but still light out enough for a walk. We must loan one of our friends a jacket, and this loan seems a kind of extension, a club jacket, a grant of temporary membership. We walk in pairs, us ahead.

We have little stories for each of the houses, we say. Don't make fun! Like, that's the house with the frowning woodpile, we say, and this is the house with the family who lives on stilts. Our friends laugh. They play along, making up names, too. These are good friends. But how ordinary the houses seem to us tonight. Two-story colonials and ranchers with cracked driveways and yards that need to be mowed. Newspapers unfolding themselves across wet lawns, their rubber bands snapped. Bikes left rusting on porches. A basketball hoop sags from stick woman's garage—how did we never notice it until now? When the jogger passes by, we wave. He waves back.

Who's that?

The jogger, we say.

The jogger, they say.

We tell them about the jogger, the man with the three-legged dog, stick woman, the two mother-daughter-sister-lesbian women, the couple with the stroller, the mailman, the kid with the stolen rollerblades, the woman who carries a cup and saucer, the man with pasty shins, the girl who dances with garden shears, the Honorary Reagans, the trampoline cat, the archery twins, the fisher of fake ponds. It grows late. Nearly dark. House lights flicker on.

It sounds like a really interesting place, our friends say. It really does. But don't you ever get a little bored?

Not really, we say.

Do you ever think you'll move back to the city?

It isn't our answer that surprises us, only its speed. Oh no, we say. We could never live anyplace where we didn't know our neighbors.

OUT LOUD

The problem with July was, Devin thought, it had no head or tail. No graduation marked its arrival, like June, when Devin had fastened his mortarboard with a bobby pin; no move would signal its close, like August, when Devin would begin his studies at a prestigious, second-tier college, saying goodbye to all that was petty, small, and beloved by his parents. "Do you know what the problem with July is?" he asked. Remi turned to look at him. "It's super hot," she said. She had her feet on the dash. Her mother had let her stick temporary butterfly tattoos on her ankles.

"No," Devin said.

"There's nothing to do?" Jules said, from the backseat.

Devin glimpsed him in the rearview mirror. He'd tied his pool towel around his neck like a cape.

"Wrong again."

"I don't like it when there's nothing to do," Jules said. He looked, for a moment, like he might cry. Devin had no idea why people thought kids were so perceptive when everything they said was stupid.

"No," Devin said, "you're both wrong." He explained to them about the head and tail.

"Can I get two ice creams today?" Jules said.

If the kids weren't so busy being morons they might actually learn something from him, Devin thought, then wondered if they'd remember their conversations later on, like in high school, when things actually started to matter.

"Can we?" Remi said.

They pulled into the pool parking lot, where other station wagons were slowing to the curb, depositing kids with limp towels tied around their waists. Devin pulled behind a minivan whose bumper sticker read WE ♥ OUR SHELTIE. For the past five weeks he'd been driving the Anderson kids to the pool. His summer job. "Be back here at three," he said.

Jules and Remi opened their doors and slunk onto the pavement. Their mother had forgotten to buy flip-flops, and the kids had to do a little dance to get to the curb. Devin saw them disappear into the pool house, pushed along, it seemed, by a current of kids in a greater rush than them, kids with better tans, thicker towels. The sight of Jules and Remi among these children never failed to rouse Devin's sense of indignation at the world, which would, he knew, run roughshod over them, while handing these other kids stock options and champagne-colored cars. The problem with the world was, Devin thought—then scraped the new speed bump he'd scraped the day before and the day before that.

Why could he never remember about that speed bump?

—

Swim practice lasted from noon until three. Devin spent his afternoon at the local book superstore. He knew it was cheesy to hang out at a book superstore, but he was trapped in a bedroom community, forty miles from any decent-sized city where, right now, people were probably making fun of everything, keen to the world's munificent shoddiness. These people, Devin imagined, might one day visit Devin's superstore. Perhaps visiting a parent or in-law, they might enter and glimpse him at the espresso bar, flipping the pages of a literary journal or zine. They'd feel sorry for him, sure, he knew that. There was no getting around that. They'd think he was a poseur, a pretender in Vans and Old Navy jeans. He wasn't trying to change that. But if they looked again, they just might spot him taking notes in his dollar-store composition book. They might notice that his pen, still wearing its umbilical cord, was stolen from the First National Bank.

Devin took a seat farthest from the magazine racks. Light slanted in from tinted windows, barring itself in diminishing rectangles across the empty tables. He had just taken his notebook from his book bag when Josie appeared.

"Howdy," he said.

"Doody," she said.

Josie held a damp rag and squirt bottle in her hand. "I haven't slept in thirty-seven hours," she said. She cleaned the table next to his. She was still wearing the leather bracelet Devin had given her for her eighteenth birthday.

"That's shutting out some shut-eye," Devin said. Immediately he felt the way he always felt around Josie: stupid, out of his league.

"My dad got back from Florida around two a.m. I picked him up at the airport. We ended up going out for waffles and talking until sunrise." She gave Devin a look. The look was meant to suggest what a burden her father was to her, but conveyed just the opposite: her barely suppressed thrill at being his caretaker and confidant.

"Wow. Those must have been some waffles." Sometimes

Devin wanted to scoop his voice from his throat and toss it into the trash.

"He wanted to talk about spiritual clarity."

"Spiritual clarity?"

"Mm. He said he'd had a vision about me. He was watching some birds along the shoreline running from the surf. You know, the way they run just ahead of the tide?"

"Right."

"Well, anyway, the birds led to a vision about him and me, so he decided to catch the next flight back and tell me all about it."

"Hm." Do not ask, Were you the birds or the ocean?

"Plus he wanted to tell me about some woman he met there. A woman named Chrysanthemum." Josie rolled her eyes.

"Sounds like a play," Devin said.

"Yeah, a tragedy," Josie said. She wiped his table, then told him she'd see him later. Devin said he was sorry about her dad, but Josie didn't say anything. It always made him feel both sad and relieved to have survived another conversation with her. They had been friends all through high school, but had recently slept together—or had they? certain technical qualifications had been left unmet—nearly ruining everything, they agreed. Devin felt guilty about it. Why did he so often feel guilty? Devin reached for his composition book. He sensed an idea coming on.

He'd purchased the composition book in response to a feature in his favorite literary magazine, *Old Scratch Robot Planet*. For months *Old Scratch* had been running a feature called "High School Out Loud," where high school students sent in their journals, diaries, e-mail correspondence, crib notes, for possible publication. Devin knew the whole concept was embarrassing (he would be the first to admit that), but couldn't help but admire the idea anyway. Plus, chances were *Old Scratch* had never seen anything as socially withering and plainly true as the notebook he was composing. Part of the genius of his notebook was the bank pen, which was quickly running out of ink, the source of a good many Nabokovian asides, as well as the composition book itself, whose pages were already wrinkled from the times he'd sat too close to the pool, Remi angling a dive toward him, or Jules chasing Big Bob with a dunked volleyball.

Big Bob. Devin hated the thought of him. Big Bob was the swim coach. Two hundred and seventy pounds, a chest like a laundry sack, he made a show of pulling the lamest swimmers around the shallow end on a life preserver. He called this activity "Big Bob's Boat," as in "Who wants to ride Big Bob's Boat?" Jules always volunteered. "Me, me!" he'd say, then hang on with the other worst swimmers in the group, waving at Devin, crying, "Look, Devin, *look*!" Devin pretended not to see him. On the day Devin had begun writing a series of observations about candy bar wrappers, he'd felt a brisk, sheeting wave across his body. Big Bob had cannonballed him from the high dive.

"How's that water feeling today?" Big Bob shouted, surfacing.

Devin gave him a grim, acknowledging smile.

"That water wet enough for you?"

Don't reach for your towel, Devin thought. Don't move.

"Who's got Big Bob's Bopper Balls?" Big Bob shouted. A group of kids instinctively ran toward a green, wooden box beneath the lifeguard post and began throwing volleyballs into the pool. Big Bob swatted these out with his fists. "Wham! Bam!" The kids chased these offerings into the link fence, where they fought over who would get to throw them back. Devin was pleased to spot Remi sitting far away from the others, drinking from a juice box. She seemed to be lost in thought, perhaps thinking of butterflies, clouds, her brother's childishness. She had her hair done up in an unusual way, Devin thought, until he realized she was too old to be Remi, then spotted the real Remi fighting Jules for a dripping volleyball. "Let go!" she cried. Jules clung to the ball, screaming, "Big Bob, help! *Big Bob*!"

"Did you see my trophy?" Jules said. "Look at my trophy." He thrust it toward Devin's face. The trophy was the size of a mouthwash cap, a miniature plastic loving cup mounted to a block whose inscription read: *To a Supershark! Hilltop Community Pool, Class 2A.* Swim practice was over. They were driving to the Purple Cow for ice cream.

"Nice," Devin said. "What did you get that for?"

Jules shrugged. "Idunno."

"You don't know?"

"Can I get two ice creams today?" Jules said.

"I think we were talking about your trophy."

"*Everyone* got one," Remi sighed. "He's just being retarded."

Jules kicked the back of Remi's seat.

"Hey, cut it out. Devin, make him cut it out."

"Cut it out," Devin said.

"But—"

"The both of you." Devin pulled into the parking lot. But instead of letting them out, Devin pressed the safety locks.

"Hey," Jules said. "No fair."

"Jules," Devin said, "I asked you a simple question, didn't I? What did you get that trophy for?"

Jules jiggled the door handle. "Idunno. For swimming and stuff."

"Do you think you deserved a trophy? I don't see your sister bragging about hers. Why is that?"

"They give them to all the kids," Remi said. "*Everybody* gets one."

"Lemme out!" Jules said. "I'm hot."

"Jules," Devin said. "Why couldn't you just answer a simple question with a simple answer? Is that too much to ask?"

Jules shrugged. "Idunno. For swimming and stuff and because."

Devin released the locks. Why bother? Minutes later the three of them were seated around a purple picnic table, Remi delicately licking peanut butter ice cream into a perfect sphere, Devin finishing his brownie sundae, and Jules munching a waffle cone, all the while staring at his trophy. The sight of him lifting the trophy toward his face like a compact mirror, again and again, filled Devin with a certain rage. "Jules," he said. "Do you really think you deserved that trophy?'

Jules shrugged. "Big Bob says I'm a Supershark."

"Jules, let me tell you something," Devin said. "Big Bob is a liar."

Jules didn't say anything.

"If you had any respect, do you know what you'd do? You'd take that trophy and throw it in the trash." Across from them, a red trash barrel sat beneath a maple tree whose bark was freckled with chewing gum. Devin waited until Jules had followed his gaze. "That's what a person with real integrity would do."

"But," Jules mumbled. "It's mine."

Here was a point Jules needed to learn. Devin could feel the air fairly crackling with learning. "No, Jules," he said. "It's everyone's and no one's at all. Do you understand?"

"It's shiny," Jules said.

"Fine," Devin said. "Keep it. Become morally hollow. Embrace the shallow, the cheap, and the easy. But a real person would throw it away."

Jules wouldn't look at him. For a moment Devin wondered if he'd gone too far—why was he always second-guessing himself? Then he and Remi watched as Jules carried the trophy to the trash can. Jules paused, making sure they were watching him.

"He won't," Remi whispered.

But he did, lowering it into a discarded drink tray. He turned to face them, then glanced back at the trash can, as if to say *See?* And they were nearly out of the parking lot before Jules pressed his face to the rear window and burst into tears. "Go back!" he cried. "I shouldn't have!" It was embarrassing, plucking the thing from the trash. And then Jules had the gall to refuse it because bees had touched it. Devin had to wipe the trophy with a damp napkin until Jules stopped crying. "Here, look," he said. "It's perfect. See? All shiny again."

Jules clutched the trophy to his chest. On the ride home, Devin could hear him whispering into its cup. "Oh, I'm sorry," he said. "I'm so sorry."

—

The next morning Devin awoke with a cold. *A cold in the summertime is like*, he wrote, *like roasting ice cubes around a campfire.* He crossed this out. *Like hearing "Deck the Halls" inside a seashell.* No. *Like wearing ski boots to the symphony.* Ski boots to the symphony? Christ, Devin thought. That didn't make any sense. Even if you thought about it for a while, it still didn't work. The problem was he was trying to be too clever. He knew that. He was aware of that. He knew what was good writing and what was bad. This was one of the many reasons he was different from everybody else, even though thinking so was a trap in itself, which might lead to a false sense of superiority. He knew that, too.

He drove to the Andersons' house. Remi and Jules were waiting on the porch. Remi was the first to notice the vitamin C tablets bulging his cheeks. "Are you okay, Devin?"

"Uh-huh," Devin said. "Shwell."

"What's wrong with you?"

Devin finished chewing. "Cold," he said.

"Are you going to die?" Jules asked.

Devin's head felt like a freshly tightened cap. "Could be," he said. He liked the way Jules looked when he said that.

"Is he really?" Jules said.

"No," Remi said.

Devin stuffed another two tablets into his mouth. "Who owes?" he said. "Dis cou be duh end."

"He's just saying that," Remi said.

"I cou be an I coudnt be. Onee time ill tell." He looked in the rearview mirror, and was pleased to register a look of fear on Jules's face.

"Are we still getting ice cream?" Jules said.

Devin dropped them off, then drove to the bookstore. The parking lot was nearly empty. The sight of Josie's car informed Devin that he didn't feel like seeing her today. He wandered around the shopping center, then stopped at a sidewalk sale, where he flipped through stacks of cut-rate coloring books. One book was *Sesame Street*–themed, but seemed to be written by someone who'd never seen the show. The Count was giving Snuffleupagus a bath in an inflatable pool while Elmo cheered them on, inexplicably, from a Zamboni. Oh, this was too good. A page later Big Bird arrived, dressed like a Viking.

Devin was about to purchase the book when he spotted Josie browsing a rack of T-shirts. She was sucking a milkshake from a tall cup (he'd forgotten how much she loved milkshakes) and was probably testing him to see how long he'd take to see her and say hi.

"Hi, Josie."

She offered a flimsy wave. "Hey."

"On break?"

"Either that or quitting forever. I haven't decided yet."

"Oh."

"Did I tell you the latest? My father wants Chrysanthemum to move in with us."

If you met Josie at the end of the world, on a bare cliff overlooking a vast, cosmic nothing, she would probably start talking about her father, Devin thought. "Geez," he said. "Sounds like a full house."

"Do you have a cold or something?"

"Yeah."

"You sound sick," Josie said.

"It's this cold."

"Oh," Josie said. She sucked down the last of the shake. "You should try vitamin C."

Devin drove to the pool. He was relieved to find he'd left his towel in the trunk. There was a bottle of Coppertone back there, too, but it had crusted over from disuse. No matter. Devin tossed it inside his book bag. A neon-orange knit cap lay beneath his father's emergency kit: it was his father's idea that Devin should wear this cap if he ever had to change a tire in the rain. It fit quite well, Devin discovered. He put his sunglasses on, popped three C's, and signed his name in the pool guest book as John Foster Dulles.

They were doing lane races. Red and blue markers had been strung across the shallow end, where Big Bob stood like a parking lot attendant, holding two flags. He gave Devin a look as Devin unfolded a deck chair and pretended to read from his notebook. They had the kids lined up in two groups. Devin could see that Remi was second in hers, Jules last in his. "Let's make some waves!" Big Bob yelled. The first two swimmers pushed off from the side. They swam past Big Bob, then stopped. "Don't stop at Big Bob!" Big Bob said. "Keep going!" The other kids joined in. "Keep going!" they screamed. The two swimmers looked at Big Bob like he was someone they couldn't quite place. "Make waves!" Big Bob yelled. The swimmers ducked back underneath the water and swam to the other side. A female lifeguard helped them out, then wrapped them in white towels.

Remi did much better. She cruised past Big Bob. Good arm strokes, strong kicks. The girl in the other lane, though, swam like swimming was a kind of game whose object was to rid the pool of its water. She flailed herself into the lane marker, stopped, then flailed into Big Bob. "Whoa," Big Bob said. "We've got a real wavemaker here." Meanwhile, Remi crossed the pool, dismissed the lifeguard's assistance, then tied a towel around her waist. Devin felt a surge of pride when he saw her help the other girl out of the pool.

A moment later Jules entered his lane.

Big Bob signaled the start.

Jules pushed off. He swam a few feet out, then drifted

sideways. His kicks were okay, no worse than the kid in the other lane, but it didn't look like he was using his arms. At all. He veered into the lane marker, crossed over, and knocked into the other swimmer. Big Bob separated them, but Jules only did the same thing again, this time breaching the second lane marker, heading toward the deep end. Big Bob carried him back to the original lane, but it was no use. Jules clung to the lane marker, out of breath. "Go! Go!" the other kids yelled. But Jules only spat water from the gap in his teeth. Finally, Big Bob scooped him onto his back, then swam him to the other side. Jules made a little show of waving the flags. Later, everyone got a chance to throw volleyballs at Big Bob as he plummeted from the high dive.

———

Jules hung his ribbon from the seat belt mount. WAVE-MAKER, the ribbon said. Remi twirled hers from her finger, bored. "I wish they weren't green," she said. "Green looks dumb."

"Can I get two ice creams today?" Jules said.

When they were seated beneath the chewing-gum tree, Devin said, "Say, Jules, what's the deal with you swimming sideways?"

Jules shrugged. His shoulder blades were like tiny hinges.

"Do you always swim sideways?"

"Idunno."

"It's because he holds his nose," Remi said. "Like this." She demonstrated. "He's scared he'll drown."

Jules protested.

"Is that the problem?" Devin asked, remembering certain childhood terrors of his own. "You're afraid you'll drown?"

"Maybe," Jules said.

"That's why Big Bob doesn't let him do Fun Swim," Remi said.

"I'm guarding the whistle!"

"He gets to guard the whistle," Remi said. "Big deal."

Devin remembered Glenview Community Pool, the summer between first and second grade. Devin's embarrassment in his fat, pale belly, lipped over his bathing trunks. Randy, his older brother, grabbing his leg, waltzing him toward the deep end. Wanting to scream, but withholding. Onlookers. Randy's friends cheering him on. They sang a song. A final breath when the water covered his ears, where, to his surprise, his heartbeat truly dwelled. Anatomy a lie. "Da-vey Jo-nes!" they sang. *Davey Jones.*

"Look," Devin said. "You're not going to drown." No, that's not it, Devin thought. Why could he never say the right thing? "I mean, it's OK that you hold your nose. For now. It's not necessarily a bad thing." Randy's expression, the day Devin swam free and pulled himself up the deep end ladder: *I've always been a little afraid of you*, it seemed to say.

"He's a baby," Remi said. "Everybody says so."

"No, you're not, Jules," Devin said. "I mean, sometimes you are, OK? I'm not going to lie about it. Sometimes you're really pathetic. You've got to admit that. But, the thing is. The thing you've got to understand is—"

Jules was looking at him like he was a flipped bus.

"Make bubbles. I guess that's what I'm saying. Hold your breath and make bubbles when you go underwater. That way you know no water is coming in."

Jules's head dimpled slightly; he sometimes chewed his tongue while thinking. "If there's bubbles?"

"Right."

"How can I see them?"

"You can't. Unless you have goggles. Do you have goggles?"

"He's *afraid* of goggles," Remi said.

"They're ouchy," Jules said.

"Doesn't matter," Devin said. "The bubbles are still there

anyway. Even if you can't see them. It's like—" he motioned with his hands. "Look, it doesn't matter what it's like. No one cares what it's like, okay? Take a big breath, bubble out, take another big breath, bubble out. Like that. Get it?"

"Bubble out," Jules said.

"Right."

"He won't remember," Remi said.

"Yes, you will," Devin said. "You'll remember."

And it wasn't until Devin drove them home, that he remembered something, too. "I got you guys something," he said. He handed Remi a crumpled bag.

"You got us presents?" Remi said.

"It's not a present," Devin said.

But Remi was already tearing away the bag. "Oh, it *is* a present!" She clutched her new pair of red flip-flops. The shoes had grown since Devin purchased them. Suddenly, they looked five sizes too large. "Thank you, Devin."

"They were on sale," Devin said. *Every small human gesture leads to an even larger human failure*, Devin thought— he'd better remember to write that one down.

Jules grabbed the blue pair and immediately started speaking into them like a telephone. "Hello?" he said. "Hello?"

"I'm not home right now," Remi said.

"Remi?" Jules said.

"Click," Remi said.

Don't let them see you blush. Think of something cool. Think of a waterfall. But all Devin could think of was the idea of a waterfall, like the ones on shampoo bottles. Had he ever really seen a waterfall? He couldn't remember.

When they reached the Andersons' house, Remi said, "Thanks again for the flip-flops." Devin told her not to worry about it. Jules opened his door, set his flip-flops on the ground, then slid his feet into them. He took two steps before tumbling onto the lawn, where he lay on his back with his pool towel splayed beside him. "Thanks, Devin," he said.

—

Devin sat on his bed, drawing stars in the margins of his composition book. The stars looked lonely without eyes and teeth, Devin thought. He fixed that, but made the mistake of trying to add bowties and clown shoes, which made the stars look like vague, shapeless blobs. *Our attempts to order the universe mock us, and ruin what is true and beautiful.* God! He crossed this out. What sophomoric trash! Forget ideas. Fuck ideas. Right. Think of people. Josie. *Likes milkshakes,* he wrote. *Strawberry. The time she got the waitress at Friendly's to hang a spoon from her nose. Her weird fear of balloons. The story about her dad making her pop them with salad tongs. Her brother who moved to Germany and sends postcards made from shopping bags.* But this didn't seem to capture Josie at all. What did he know about her, really? She liked jazz, but hated Christmas. She once kept a puppy hidden in her basement, feeding it from a bag of dog food she kept underneath her bed, thinking her parents wouldn't know. She'd never been to Kentucky.

What did he know about anything, really? The time they'd nearly slept together Josie started crying before they were even undressed. "What's wrong?" Devin asked.

"Nothing," Josie said. But she didn't stop crying. She held her hands to her face. Her shoulders trembled.

"Are you angry at me?"

Josie wiped her face. "No," she said.

"I didn't mean to make you upset."

"It's not that," Josie said.

"You know we don't have to do anything."

"I know," Josie said. "It's not that." She looked at him, and tried to smile. But it was the opposite of a smile. "Well," she said, touching a finger to the bulge in his jeans, "you're definitely a boy."

That had been the week before he visited the college campus, where he and his parents took a guided tour. The guide led them to the library, whose empty aisles and high-ceilinged reading room gave Devin a lonely feeling, as did the dining hall, where he was saddened to see the same lunch trays and drinking cups they used in his high school cafeteria. The dormitories gave off an odor of damp towels and had beds stacked on top of cinderblock risers. He would have to sleep in these beds. He would have to eat off these trays. He would be lonely here, he saw. How had he never realized this before? He walked back to his parents' car with a feeling like he was slowly being lowered into a hole.

"It's such a pretty campus," his mother said.

"Wish I could move in today," Devin said.

What did he know about anything?

—

The next afternoon, Devin dragged a deck chair to the edge of the pool where Big Bob was stringing lane markers across the shallow end. The sun made pleasing, paisley shapes on the water, which chuckled when it entered the skimmer near Devin's feet. Big Bob spotted him and swam close. "Professor Notebook," he said. "That your name?"

Devin shrugged.

"Should be," Big Bob said. His nose was thickly striped with Desitin. "Oh, Professor Notebook, oh, oh," he sang, then swam away.

A few moments later Remi swam toward him. "Devin?" she said. "What are you doing sitting so close? You're not supposed to—" a lap of water finished her sentence. The poor kid.

"Is there a law against sitting this close?"

"Well, no. But—"

"Well, then, there we have it. Let's say I'm a lawful lounger, right?"

"I guess."

And when Remi pulled herself out of the water, a solid minute before the girl in the other lane, Devin handed her a towel. "Thanks, D-Devin," she said. Her teeth chattered.

"Where's Jules?" Devin asked.

"G-guarding the whistle."

Devin approached Jules. He was sitting beneath the lifeguard stand, twirling the whistle above his head and making helicopter noises. Jules spotted him, and immediately hid the whistle behind his back. "Hey, Devin," he said.

"Hey."

The two of them watched the other kids race, heard cheers, laughter.

"So, that's the whistle?" Devin said.

"Yeah."

"Can I see it?"

Jules considered this. "But I'm supposed to guard it." The lifeguard stand cast shadows across his body.

"I know," Devin said. "I won't take it. I promise."

Jules handed him the whistle. It was the kind Devin's kindergarten gym teacher had used when they played dodgeball indoors. A gray rope grew from its top, long as a necklace. "You know, Jules," Devin said, "I could probably guard this whistle for a while. I mean, if you wanted to swim or anything."

"But I'm supposed to guard it," Jules said.

Don't point out that he just said that. "I know," Devin said. "I understand. But you could deputize me, swim a little, then get the whistle back."

"Deputize?"

Disregard the annoying way he's putting his feet together, like a gimp bird. "Sure. That way you're still guarding the whistle, but swimming, too." Devin looked away, feigning indifference. "You know, you'd probably be the first person to ever do that."

Jules's strokes weren't much better than before, but he managed to make it out to Big Bob, who seemed surprised to find him passing by. He crouched down, offering a ride, but Jules refused. Was it the way the sunlight hit the pool, or did Jules seem a bit taller, shaking his head no? Devin had never watched the races with his sunglasses off; perhaps this accounted for the illusion that Jules was swimming with twice his normal speed, his legs finding a rhythm. Big breaths, Devin thought. Bubble out. There was a word to describe the feeling

Devin had, seeing Jules arrive at the opposite end where Devin now stood, waiting. And it wasn't until Devin lifted Jules from the water, his skinny wrists almost nothing in his hands, that he realized what word it was: *weightless.*

TORO

When Jonas was nine, the job of mowing the lawn fell to him and offered, like the binoculars his father left behind, a magnified view of the world. The lawn, which had always seemed to him a dull carpet where horseshoes could be pitched, sprinklers hopped, and footballs made to stand on end, now revealed itself to be the stage upon which the house actually stood, whose proper care was a kind of drama in which Jonas, pushing the mower with socks rolled to his ankles, became his father's sudden understudy. Neighbors, spotting him, waved. Bees, indifferent to the mower's path, lingered. How had his father negotiated the hydrangea bush?

The mower, a self-propelled push job, was difficult to start. Dry grass caked the roof of its mouth; Jonas chiseled it away with a screwdriver. A mower, underneath, was really not much at all, he discovered. Oil, previously imagined precious, like gold, actually came in squat bottles with necks like pulled balloons. A funnel was needed for the gasoline; filling it was a kind of game. Jonas's hands shook from the effort. A T-topped pull cord grew from the motor's head, like Frankenstein's bolt, Jonas thought, then grew angry at himself for thinking that. Twice already that summer he'd woken from sleep convinced that a convict had a gun to his ear, when really it was his pillow's zipper pressing against his side. Lightning was not, he reminded himself, aiming for his window. His house was just his house in darkness or in light. The lawn was just a lawn. The mower just a mower. Why, then, did the mower seem to know something? Why did it feel, on those summer evenings when he'd waited until the sun had nearly set, as if it were trying to hurry him along? OK, OK, Jonas said, following the mower around the lip of the flower bed, whose wood chips he had often used to draw four-square courts on the driveway, and whose border the mower seemed to honor, like a car at a crosswalk.

The lawn had its own geography, unknown to him all those years of running, playing catch. The grass along the driveway wasn't really grass at all, but a kind of hay that must have grown there accidentally. The grass around the mailbox grew especially thick; he would have to use the yellow clippers tacked to the garage wall, the ones he had once used to cut a pizza box into the moons of Jupiter, a class project whose purpose was now lost to memory. He would need gloves for this. Gloves, in summer. The lawn pulled seasons inside out. The grass near the front porch was soft as fine hair, perhaps something to do with the shadow of the house, Jonas guessed. The side yard sloped more steeply than he had remembered, tugging the mower forward. The ground near the air-conditioning unit always felt soggy underfoot. Why?

If the lawn was wet, the mower breathed tiny wisps of smoke.

Dry, the mower turned dandelions into wishes.

Daytime mowings embarrassed Jonas, with cars passing by, seeing him stopped before a stalk of ragweed, waiting for wasps to take flight. He didn't like to sweat, something new to him, as were the showers he took afterward, forgoing the tub, which had gladly swallowed his dirt for years now, its greedy drain finishing with a satisfied ah! The shower cared less, somehow. Now, its spout seemed to say. Now, now! The water stung Jonas's face and pinked his shoulders. But when Jonas lifted his chin, he found a surprise: the water could be taken in the mouth, gargled, and noisily spit wherever. From this knowledge, came another: all the water in the house was the same water and did not know which kind of water it was. Jonas, after deliberation, allowed himself to pee into the drain.

At his mother's request, Jonas kept a log book of all his mowings for allowance purposes. The notebook had a speckled cover and a wide, white nameplate where Jonas blocked in his name, putting LAWN in the space for "Grade," and MOWINGS in the space for "Semester." It bothered him to leave the space for "Homeroom" empty, like a painted-over window, so he wrote the name of the lawnmower there, TORO, pleased with the idea of someone finding the book later on. He kept the book inside his nightstand, sometimes thumbing through it before bed, reviewing his stats. He had mowed on every day of the week except Wednesday and had twice mowed on holidays, Good Friday and Memorial Day. He rarely mowed on Tuesday. Saturday was the hands-down winner. Longest stretch without: thirteen days. This, a vacation with his school friend, Alex Gregg, at the Greggs' beach house, which, the notebook reminded him, had been a disappointment. They'd walked the beach with flip-flops pinching their toes, T-shirts damp at the hems, spying on girls and rolling their R's, a school joke that no longer seemed funny to Jonas, as did Alex's impression of Mr. Bowden, their homeroom teacher. "So what do you think?" Alex had asked, lifting his shirt and drumming his pale belly. "You think chicks will wanna lick this six-pack?" Nights, Jonas slept on a fold-out bed, feeling, for the first time, the kind of loneliness particular to houses where the pantry is stocked with cookies, chips, and soda, and all along the stairway, family photographs hang like bright glass.

But how boring mowing was. Such magnificent nothing! Such shapelessness! The lawn had no head or tail; Jonas would fix that. If he began with the strip of grass along the road, that was the "front" of the lawn, or, imagined from above, the "top." Moving horizontally, then, toward the house made the side yard the "middle," and the last few rows beneath the back deck, where Jonas was afraid to duck underneath, as he had seen his father do, must be the "back" or "bottom." What about the other side yard, though? The driveway side with a collapsed woodpile rotting at its base, bee-ridden and smelling of damp leaves. Jonas always saved it for last, hurrying through. He had never played there, even when they'd first moved in. Unlike the air conditioner side, this side—the opposite side, Jonas thought—was not a passageway to another yard, nor could you cross from the front yard to the back, unless you hopped the woodpile, which seemed to Jonas a kind of cheating, like dragging your pencil through the wall of a maze. He finished there by mowing a square pattern that diminished into smaller squares upon smaller squares until all that was left was one square less than the width of the lawnmower, which the mower happily accepted into its maw, the motor surging as the blades spun free. If Jonas thought of these squares as a curled tail, like the ones worn by monkeys in his favorite video game, then this would allow the side yard its proper place in the body of the lawn. Finishing with a tail. The idea pleased him.

But mowing was slow, repetitive. The lawn, seen through the mower's handles, repeated itself frame after frame, like empty slides in a carousel. Grass, green in storybooks, photographs, and dreams, in truth nurtured yellow buds and yellow-brown stalks, whose tops turned purple when left to grow too long, and emerged from the underside of Jonas's mower slickly transparent like the wings of a fly. In the shade, grass appeared black. A consolation: blades of grass were exactly that, sharp to the touch, when Jonas rubbed them from his legs, pausing beneath the shade of the house while the mower spun its wheels—he had maintained, too, his father's fastidiousness. After each mowing, he left his grass-mowing sneakers in the garage, their bottoms wetly green like halved limes. This leaving, too, part of a repetition, as was the feeling, when Jonas dared to push the mower underneath the back deck, of someone trying to call his name. A trick of the enclosed space, Jonas figured, without actually believing it. Unaware, he'd had the exact same thought every time he'd mowed around the mailbox, a memory of a puzzle he and his cousin had once vainly tried to assemble atop a picnic table, the table sheltered within a park gazebo whose roof hung five curtains of rainwater around them, the puzzle missing several key pieces, the rain sometimes blowing in. The sense of their mission, its hopelessness, had stayed with him in dreams, car rides, and now in the stubborn grass around the mailbox's pole that when edged, caught the mower's wheels and caused the handle to shake. Jonas had twice taken the same number of steps to finish the side yard.

There were problems with mowing. The lawn needed cutting when Jonas least felt like it, for one. For another, dog shit. One time Jonas mowed over a rabbit burrow, releasing three baby bunnies, each taking off in a different direction. He'd tried placing the rabbits back into the burrow, but they pushed through the flimsy grass roof he'd dropped on top of them. An idea: he topped the burrow with a trash can lid, weighting it with a rock. When he'd lifted it again, afraid that they'd suffocate, he found the burrow empty. He put his hand inside the hole, feeling its grassy nothing.

The lawn made him complicit in miracles. Mysteries.

If it rained for several days, Jonas was unable to mow without the mower blades getting stuck. The lawn, sensing its advantage, sent up unlikely foliage to mock Jonas. Red vines appeared from behind the air-conditioning unit, their leaves hooking the underside of the machine. Purple flowers drooped from the ends of a weed whose roots made a sound like cloth tearing when Jonas pulled them from the side yard. White mushrooms appeared at the base of the woodpile, like trolls.

Like vines, lawn problems clung to something larger. For months Jonas had been troubled by a hitch in his infrequent prayers, whereby praying for one person begged praying for another, until there was always a displaced person, hopelessly left out, looking in through the fence of his attention. If Jonas thought *And please watch over Mom and Dad, Grandmom and Grandpop and Mom-Mom*, this left out Pop-Pop, who died when Jonas was five and who had once taken Jonas on a tour of a historical battlefield where Jonas was allowed to press buttons on glassed museum displays in which toy soldiers described bloody battles that looked perfectly pleasant to Jonas, with everyone dressed in smart caps and roped jackets, riding muscular horses into blue streams. *And Pop-Pop, too*, Jonas prayed, including him among the loved and living, but displacing Uncle Al, who showed up only at Christmas, like eggnog, and cousin Cathy, from Ohio and pretty, whose presence in these prayers only made it clear that Jonas loved cousin Michael and Aunt Frida and Aunt Stephanie less. These unlucky few congregated behind the fence with Kevin Forrester and Chris Orner, school friends displaced by Josh Boyd and Jim Stevens, neighborhood pals, whose bedrooms Jonas had slept in and whose sinks had accepted his spit.

Likewise, the lawn made displacements. If Jonas tried to align the left edge of the mower along the indentation left by his first pass, he sometimes strayed, leaving an archipelago of uncut grass between the rows, requiring him to double back, fixing it. But these repairs tugged the right-hand margin of uncut grass to the left, requiring Jonas to repeat the mistake over and over again for the sake of continuity. If Jonas concentrated, the mistake could be corrected within two passes, simply by starting a new, mistake-free margin just to the left or right of the ragged one, and following it across. But the correction involved a kind of wastefulness that bothered Jonas, who had acquired his father's habit of tearing scrap paper into reusable quarters and stacking them by the downstairs telephone. For every corrected row hid the broken one underneath, and made the expenditure of the second pass appear thrifty, pennywise. Jonas watched the jagged edge spool itself beneath the mower's front, feeling vaguely guilty but clever, too. He gripped the mower's handle and felt sweat trickle past his ear.

But Jonas could not concentrate. His thoughts—something happened to them while he mowed. They broke. They hid. Jonas tried to score them with a Walkman, but the Toro's motor was too noisy, no matter how high he turned the volume or how well Jonas could follow the songs without actually hearing them. This truth revealed another one: it was just as good to think of songs as to listen to them. Better, even.

So Jonas did. He started with a record, pulled from its staticky sleeve, placed on the dual-drive turntable he was only recently allowed to use, whose top could be lifted with the side of his hand, the record making a pleasing, plunking sound when dropped onto the platter, whose sides were illuminated by an amber strobe. Through some optical trick, the platter's banding looked like it was moving in opposite directions, like a helicopter's propeller. It was these bands that Jonas imagined when he pulled the mower's cord from its head, starting both machines, as it were, one imagined, one real, Jonas's first steps across the driveway the leader groove on side one. The mower, then, the stylus "playing" the grass grooves. Jonas edged the mower along the front porch, singing.

Why then, with songs to cheer him, did the back deck frighten him? The ground beneath it sloped upward, softly, always damp, even on the hottest of days, which troubled Jonas's footing and made him feel as if he might fall. Was that it? Or was it the lone wasp's nest hanging like a brown disco ball from the beam above the basement door? His first time mowing, Jonas had nearly walked right into it; he'd run away so quickly he was in the neighbor's yard, looking back, before the image of the nest, its papery shell tapering to a single hole from which two wasps descended in the moment Jonas had released the Toro's handle, returned to him in utter clarity, the wasps' black legs dangling from their bodies like tucked hairs. He'd left the mower underneath the deck until after dark, when he figured the wasps would be sleeping—did wasps sleep?—then pulled it out and dragged it back to the garage, his heart pounding.

He was also afraid of the weeds behind the front porch rainspout, whose leaves were shiny, like poison ivy, and from which he had once seen a garter snake emerge, racing along the house wall and, Jonas imagined, working its way into the plumbing so that it might wait inside a toilet. A dark green circle marked the spot in the lawn where Jonas had once buried a robin inside a cookie tin, and this spot, too, bothered Jonas, since he remembered lining the tin with paper towels, when he should have used cloth napkins, or at least an old shirt. Did the robin hold it against him? Jonas, when mowing over it, said, "Sorry."

Jonas's house, which he had always imagined as a kind of fortress, was really nothing of the kind. Cracks fanned from corners of basement windows, like squints. The siding beneath Jonas's bedroom was missing two strips, a third hanging out, like a pouch. A brown dampness clung to the base of the chimney where weeds grew from between the bricks. What was worse, the house wore some of its organs on the outside, like the gray electric box that sat beneath the dining room window, with two gray wires climbing the wall; the electric meter visibly crouching behind the hydrangea bush, its head eyed with white dials. Jonas had tried to decipher them once, but it was like trying to read the stock page, as his father used to do, and which he sometimes attempted when no one was around. Anyone could read these dials, these vital signs. Anyone could cut these wires or smash these boxes, which made a slight thrumming noise, as did the electric wires which sloped toward the lawn, then disappeared into the ground, mysteriously skirted with weeds. As if to prove the house's vulnerability, Jonas once saw a white truck park itself in their driveway, and a black-booted man emerge with a clipboard and a measuring stick, which he promptly stuck into the hole Jonas believed might be a passageway to Narnia. The man looked at the stick, wrote something on the clipboard, then dropped the heavy lid back into place. Spotting Jonas mowing the lawn, he offered him a wave. When Jonas waved back, the man smiled, then saluted him.

If the house was less substantial than it was supposed to be, Jonas thought, then being inside was little different from being outside. He had had the same feeling during his last trip to the dentist, whose office used to be a house, a sootless fire-place in the waiting room, a business sign hanging from the front porch. Inside, a little sink swirled blue water into itself, endlessly, in a room where meals must have once been eaten, coats hung on pegs. Here Jonas bit down on a foam mouth-piece gelled with bright paste and later placed his chin against a fixed perch while a camera—the dental assistant kept call-ing it "Pinocchio"—peered into his jaw. All of these things happened in rooms where windows looked out onto a lawn, greener and more neatly manicured than Jonas's own. Jonas felt the dentist's fingers pressing against his lips and watched a lawn crew at work. Had someone once looked out this win-dow, feeling the satisfaction of a freshly mowed lawn, as Jonas often did? His bedroom now seemed like the backside of the window where cut grass sometimes stuck, and where the sun lingered, on those evenings when Jonas raced it, picking up his pace. The basement no longer a strong vault, secret to the world, but a flimsy box sealed within the lawn. All the first-floor rooms—kitchen, dining, living, and family—a wall away from fat ladybugs climbing gray milkweed. Sometimes Jonas allowed himself to push the Toro into the garage while it was still running, letting it pass over oil stains and tire marks, the motor's noise like the house was holding a note. *Jonas*, his mother mouthed, opening the kitchen door, and covering the phone with her hand. *I'm on the phone.* Jonas cut the engine, but the sound rang in his ears and followed him into the house, where it accompanied the removal of his socks, from which shavings fell, bringing the lawn into his bedroom.

———

One day a neighbor stopped Jonas as he began edging the grass around the mailbox. "You've got to change your pattern," he shouted. "It's drying up your lawn." He held out his hand and demonstrated a vertical line, then horizontal, diagonal, criss-cross. "Makes a world of difference." Jonas considered this. For weeks he'd been mowing less—a gap in the log book—while the grass dried and drank sprinkler water like a colander beneath a running tap. So he began with the side yard, the monkey's tail, and worked his way out into the back yard, which he now crossed diagonally. The new angle tugged his attention toward his neighbors' yards, fences, houses, and patios. Beyond them, trees. Beyond the trees, roads with cars hugging corners, trucks air braking. These places were closer than he had imagined, Jonas realized, his neighbors' windows affording a full view of him pushing the Toro toward them. Certainly people had watched him mow without him knowing it. Certainly people had seen him filling the mower with gas. The stage that he had imagined facing in, in truth faced out. A magnified world could also be viewed from the opposite end of the binoculars. Jonas, sensing an audience, picked up his pace and neglected the grass beneath the deck.

PARADE REST

We're outside, spit-shining marching band cymbals, when Randy the Raven shows up. We both know it's Pete Hampson inside, but that doesn't make much difference, really. Pete's wearing his mascot head with its creepy wide eyes, his breath like a runner crossing the finish line. We used to be friends, Pete and I. Back in middle school. But we never mention this anymore. I am fifteen, a cymbal player in the school marching band. My best friend is Larry Greer. It was Larry's idea to shine the cymbals outside, to get the best possible light. Tonight our football team is playing its homecoming game.

"You boys rubbing it up?" Pete says.

"For the game," Larry says.

"The game," Pete says. "You two like to play games?" He

puts his sneaker against the twenty-inch crash I've been buffing to a shine. I've always hated the way you can see Randy the Raven's sneakers poking through the bottom of his costume. Like a kid hiding behind a curtain. Ruins the effect.

"The football game," Larry says. Larry still collects action figures, although I am keeping this a secret under penalty of blackmail, since Larry knows I cried a little at the end of *E.T.*

"Rubbing it up for the big game, eh?" Behind Pete, I see Christie Alrich and Ashley Orr walk by carrying silk flags. Ashley gives Pete a punch on the shoulder. "Be nice," she warns.

"Randy the Raven loves all," Pete says.

"We're supposed to make them shine like mirrors," Larry explains. These are the words of our band director, Mr. Phillips.

But Pete isn't listening. He's watching Jennifer and Ashley. "*I'm* nice," he says. A moment later he removes his mascot head, beneath which his bushy hair has conformed to the shape of Randy's cranium, a half-moon or inverted bowl. "We know we're cool, right fellas?" Pete extends a hand to me. "Like, it's all good and whatnot?"

"I guess," I say.

"I'm OK, you're OK?"

"I guess."

"Because Timex takes a licking, but keeps on ticking," Pete says. "And that's a fact, Jack."

Here is my problem: I have no idea what to do anymore. Should I grab Pete by the leg and swing him to the ground? Or should I say, "And that's a fact, Jack!" the way we used to when we were in middle school? Or should I act totally bored, not say anything at all, suggesting I'm holding tremendous wisdom in reserve? I've always wanted to be that kind of person. But what I end up doing is saying, "That's way back, Jack!" A laugh escapes my lips like a squeezed toy.

"Whatever," Pete says. A moment later he's gone and I'm left with Larry, who should be mad at me, who should be seriously thinking about breaking off and finding some first-class, grade-A friendship, but of course isn't, because he's Larry and because really, who else is going to be friends with him?

"Pete's a good mascot," he says.

I don't say anything.

"Lots of energy."

I'll become a stone, I think. Sinking to the bottom of a deep pond, heavy with dignity.

"Plus he's tall," Larry says. He holds a cymbal to the sun, inspecting it. "Everybody likes a tall mascot."

—

I live with my mom and stepfather, Frank. Frank is fourteen years older than my mother. He's a self-employed accountant with one daughter from his first marriage. Jennifer. They don't see each other all that much, but last Christmas Jennifer came to visit, my mother's idea. Jennifer was just finishing up college in Montana. The four of us had sat around our dining-room table, trying to think of things to say, while Nat King Cole sang from our old Fisher stereo, the one Larry likes to tinker with whenever he's over here. The table was fitted out with red and green placemats, wreaths of holly, and the same snowmen candles we've used every Christmas since forever. I couldn't stop looking at the snowmen, their ruddy cheeks, their doffed stovepipe hats, underneath which blackened wicks grew like renegade cowlicks. The kind of thing you can't help but notice when you've finished up on seconds of mashed potatoes and crescent rolls and the only sound is your mother saying, for the third time that evening, "Must get pretty cold in Montana."

Jennifer stayed in my bedroom while I took the couch in the living room. All night the Christmas tree blinked its blinky cheer for me. From the couch I could hear Jennifer using the bathroom, whose door has always creaked like a pirate's chest. I heard her getting back into to bed. I didn't know then that Jennifer would end up moving in with us after graduation. No job prospects, she said. Just a short stay to get her things in order. A summer job to earn a little extra money. I didn't know then that Jennifer would stay on with us into the fall, sending out resume after resume from our crooked mailbox, whose exterior she painted bright lavender with white daisies. I didn't know the living room couch would become my bed.

I started spending more time at Larry's house. After school we'd hang out in his driveway and shoot baskets while his dog, Tex, napped on the free throw line Larry had chalked seven feet too close to the hoop. I'd dribble past Tex, release the ball, all the while thinking of ways to end my friendship with Larry. I had several ideas. Most of these involved me getting a girlfriend. I imagined her to be quiet with dark hair and librarian glasses, surprisingly pretty when she wore contact lenses and laughed at my incredibly nuanced impersonation of Larry. It was terrible, not having a girlfriend. But my prospects weren't very good, and Larry's were even worse, which seemed another depressing proof of our compatibility. We'd play until it grew dark, then go inside, where Larry's parents greeted me like I was a celebrity. Sometimes Larry's dad would let us drive his Volkswagen around the block.

I could not think of Jennifer as my girlfriend. I tried to, early on, but whatever illusions I had were dispelled by spending time with her. We had nothing in common. Plus she had a boyfriend back in Montana, Steve, although she was reluctant to talk about him. Jennifer liked to watch westerns—westerns!—and read magazines about horses. She loved horses. She had a horse back in Montana, but had to sell him when she left for college. You wouldn't believe how much it costs to keep a horse, she said. I told her I couldn't imagine. But Jennifer was OK. Once I gave up on her I actually found myself liking her well enough. She could make a pretty good joke every once in a while and she seemed genuinely interested in how I was doing in school, was there anyone I liked? And she liked Larry, which took some of the pressure off when he came over. They'd hang out at the kitchen table, drinking Dr. Pepper and reading horse magazines while Larry asked her questions about stables, feed, bridles. Larry said he'd always wanted to see Montana. He had an idea that Montana was the place for him.

Larry was adopted. His birth parents had given him up when he was a baby; he didn't know much about them. Didn't want to know.

"How could you not want to know?" I asked, one weekend when I was staying over.

"Not interested."

"They'd probably look like you."

"I guess."

"I'd want to see if they looked like me," I said.

Larry shrugged.

"I'd want to talk to them without them knowing," I said. I could almost picture it, me, a waiter at a fancy restaurant overlooking a city skyline, my birth parents asking me about the specials. A white towel draped across my arm, their eager faces turned toward mine. "Then I'd lay it on them—boom! See what they'd have to say for themselves."

"My parents are my parents," Larry said.

Larry's parents were the oldest parents of anyone I knew. Grandparent old. Larry's mom had false teeth; his father hoarded milk jugs full of pennies along the basement stairs, convinced they would one day be collector's items. Sometimes Larry and I would dump the pennies out onto the basement floor, just because. It was amazing how precious they seemed. The newer coins like tiny jewels. Lincoln's head worn to almost nothing on the oldest ones. I held one to the light whose weight had been doubled by a skin of green dross. We found hundreds bundled into tight paper tubes, the coins refusing to separate when we shucked them from their wrapping.

"We'll be millionaires," Larry said.

It bothered me the way Larry acted around his parents. He laughed at his dad's corny jokes and lousy puns. He washed and rewashed a personalized coffee mug his mother had given him for his eleventh birthday, drinking every drink from behind its oversized handle, whose top Larry pinched with his bent thumb. It was embarrassing the way he allowed his mother to knead his topcoat with a lint roller when we were already late for band practice. Sometimes his parents watched us from the bleachers, applauding the dumbest things. They'd whistle when Larry and I marched to the fifty-yard line to offer our clasped cymbals as hi-hats to the drumline. "That your parents?" Mike Kohl asked as we stood at attention, the song over.

"Yup," Larry said.

"Your dad's waving a thermos," Mike said.

Larry smiled. "What's my mom doing?"

"She's eating a pretzel—wait. Now she's waving the pretzel."

I wanted Larry to have some cynicism. Or at least some angst. Everyone else I knew had plenty to spare. Hell, we were practically *ordered* to be cynical by every movie, TV show, song, book, video game aimed at us. *Slouch—now!* the world seemed to say. *Or else!*

These, my thoughts the band practice before the homecoming game. A Thursday night, outdoors beneath the stadium lights. Larry marching beside me, counting aloud, twenty-four measures of rest until we raise our cymbals, my entrance at measure twenty-five, beat two, announcing the trumpet fanfare, Larry at measure twenty-six, shadowing the bass drums. It's the lowliest thing, being a cymbal player, but harder than you'd think, too. All that waiting around. All that marching to nothing. You'd think Larry would know the score by now, but I think he likes the idea of counting aloud. Like he's the one conducting. I do stuff like that too, sometimes, but I would never tell Larry this.

Practice begins with our entrance into the stadium. We line up in twos, instruments at our side, and march from the school parking lot onto the field, our feet keeping time with the drum cadence, a martial beat that reaches a crescendo when we've assembled along the visitor's sideline, where we stand shoulder to shoulder trying to suppress the urge to laugh. It's the hardest thing, not laughing. It's this sudden, joyful-awful feeling, like fearing you're about to shout during a funeral. Never do we stand so close together. Hallways packed tight between classes offer the veil of purpose; we must get to algebra, to social studies, to lunch. Even the bus affords enough room to spread your coat across the backseat, declaring Mine. Reserved. Gym class, a hurried pass with your parents' bath towel, slipping on your jeans in two seconds flat, not looking at all the not looking occurring around you. Brushing against someone's arm an affront requiring immediate apology. Sorry.

The drum major calls us to attention.

Band! Ten-hut!

We snap our heels together—*Hut!*

The drum major performs his salute to the benefit of empty stands. This also funny, but we do not laugh. The major feigns surprise when Randy the Raven hijacks his baton and starts playing it like a guitar. Hands on hips, the major admonishes the silly bird, whose head shakes in remorse as he hands the baton over, the first trumpet playing a muted *wah-wah* as Mr. Phillips has advised. But Randy is undeterred: he lines up like a center ready to snap a phantom ball, when the major calls us to attention again.

Band! Instruments up!

And then the opening bars of "Sunfire Tempest," us marching out onto the field, the trombones trampling poor Randy, who dusts himself off, then does a cartwheel at midfield. Larry and I shadow the percussion section, following the bass drums for the first half of the song, then march alongside the snares for the big finale. There's a moment when Larry and I separate, him part of an eighth note's flag that materializes at the forty-yard line, me part of a sixteenth at the thirty-five. I see him disappear behind a row of tubas, whose bells have been capped with red and white letters. For a moment Larry is gone. Adios! Then I see him again, marching toward me, his mouth moving to the count. His glasses have slipped askew, feet out of step. The plume atop his cap tugs the brim too far forward. We meet at the forty-five, facing each other.

"Twenty-one, two, three, four; twenty-two, two, three, four," Larry counts.

And this is when I realize I've lost the count. Gone. But Larry's carrying it to me, a relayed baton. We perform a smooth exchange. I raise my cymbals. Then:

"—*!*"

The sound a struck bell is suffered to hear. A thousand sudden released breaths. If sunflowers could scream.

The cymbals quiver in my hands, straining against their leather straps. The feeling lasts an amazingly long time. Sometimes I can still feel it during the rests, the cymbals not quite held to my sides, the moment before I pull them in and snuff them out.

But here's the thing: Larry. He's still there, next to me. The inescapable fact of him. And there goes my reverie—poof! What to do about Larry? This, the thought all my others tend toward. No matter what. As in:

"I think I'll eat the last of the Nutter Butters." = Nutter Butters-cookies-sugar-flour-peanuts-kitchen-drawer-packaging-torn-plastic tray-broken-crumbs-plate or napkin?-neither-stand over sink-wash evidence away-bury package-trash-coffee grinds-newspaper-onion peels-onions-round-misshapen-Larry's head-Larry-What to do about Larry?

Or:

"Guess I'll wear my winter coat today." = Too warm?-torn hem-carry instead-heavy-stuff in locker-hallway-school-Larry-What to do about Larry?

Or:

"Great day!" = But?-*Larry!*

We march through the next number, a big band tune no one likes, then launch into our finale, a "Yesterday-Hey Jude-Let It Be" medley our band director has arranged. It doesn't sound too bad, but takes forever, all those "Hey Jude" nah-

nah-nah-nah's climbing over one another, while Larry and I crash on two and four, windmilling the cymbals toward the stadium lights, an effect Larry's mother swears is beautiful. The piece ends with Larry and me stuck in front of the percussion section, close to the stands. It's humiliating, this part of the routine. I can see just about everyone. Parents and friends, teachers. Kids whose gazes I've spent the past two years avoiding. Concession stand workers. Larry's dad. I see them all looking beyond us, the moment before Larry and I turn and face the band. The song ends. Applause. The drum major blows a whistle, then commands parade rest.

Band! Pa-rade rest!

Parade rest. Shoulders back, feet apart.

Hut!

Silence. I can see the entire band. I can see the drumline, their yellow berets slipped to one side; the trumpeter whose shoe never fails to slip free; the twirler posing with a phantom baton, the real in the grass at her feet. The feeling of seeing everyone at rest is almost too much. A feeling like passing through a neighborhood at night and glimpsing, in one brightly lit window, a woman standing at the kitchen sink; in another, two children watching television. A thrilling and disappointing intimacy. I know something of these people, but almost nothing about them. Close strangers. Nameless kin.

Afterward, Larry and I ride in the backseat of his father's Volkswagen. Larry and his father keep passing a rubber squeeze toy whose eyes and lips bulge with every squeeze.

"*Blah!*" Larry says, holding the thing to my face.

"Nice," I say.

Then Larry holds it to the window, squeezing it at other drivers. "Excuse me," he says in this lousy British accent, "but would you happen to have any *blah!*?"

This cracks Larry's father up. "Please, sir," he says, "we'll have no *blah!* in this vehicle."

"Terribly sorry, old chap," Larry says. "Please accept my most sincere apologies for *blah!*"

Up close, the toy smells like a wet tennis ball. I think about having my own car. I think about next year, becoming an entirely different person. I think about throwing the toy off an overpass. So why do I feel a slight twinge of regret when, a mile from home, the thing's head pops like an overinflated balloon?

"Oh no," Larry says.

"Let me see," his father says.

Larry hands the toy over.

"Well," his father sighs, "at least we got a few good squeezes out of him."

—

The night of the homecoming game, Jennifer's boyfriend shows up, the one from Montana. Steve. He's sitting on the couch reading a magazine when I get back from school.

"The phone rang," he says, "just before you came in. I thought I would tell you." He's got the blanket I use at night draped across his shoulders. "Jennifer's in the shower," he explains.

We introduce ourselves. We shake hands. "Thanks," I say.

"For a second I thought I should answer it," Steve says. "Then I felt guilty when I didn't." He gives me a look like he's just said something amusing, then goes back to the magazine. "Isn't that funny? But maybe they left a message."

They did. Larry, telling me his dad can't drive us to the game. Could Jennifer? Could I ask?

This, another crime of being fifteen: you always need a ride. Always. I tried walking to practice once, but gave up after leaving my neighborhood. It wasn't the distance that stopped me; it was the idea of everyone seeing me walking along the highway.

"We can't," Jennifer says. "We're going to a movie."

"Sure, we could," Steve says. He's making us hot chocolate from this tin of baking cocoa we've had since I was in junior high. I could never figure out how to make hot chocolate from baking cocoa. "We've got plenty of time."

"Steve," Jennifer says. She gives him a look.

"Think of it as an adventure," Steve says.

The hot chocolate is amazing. All this time, sitting in the pantry. I've always liked it when someone visits your house and discovers something you couldn't care less about, saying, Look at *this*.

"We have to pick up Larry," I say.

"See?" Steve says. "We have to pick up Larry."

"Fine," Jennifer sighs. "Whatever."

And, just like that, the evening starts to organize itself around Steve. A feeling like raking leaves into a single pile. Like that we're putting on our coats and climbing into Jennifer's Honda. Like that I'm pushing aside empty water bottles and fast food bags, Jennifer apologizing, Steve taking the driver's seat, which slides back into my knees. Steve drives with his window down. I can see the wind taking his hair, too long around his ears, wanting a trim. I don't know how to explain it, but Steve doesn't seem like someone from Montana. Not to me, at least. For one thing, he's got wire-rimmed glasses; for another, he's not wearing boots. He has a habit of finishing his sentences with a slight intake of breath, as in "This is a good little car (ah). Really lets you know you're driving (ah)." I can't see him roping a calf.

When we get to Larry's house, Larry is standing on his front porch, already dressed in his band uniform. It always embarrasses me when he does that. He's even wearing his hat, firmly strapped underneath his chin.

"You look like you're about to storm a bunker," Steve says.

"This is Steve," Jennifer explains.

"I've seen pictures," Larry says.

We drive out of the neighborhood where porch lights are just winking into life. Steve and Larry immediately lock into a discussion about Spain, where Steve was an exchange student for a semester. Larry wants to know if you're looking at the Atlantic ocean from Spain, does it feel like you're looking at it the wrong way? Steve tells him about a wild cab ride in Barcelona. Larry counters with a story about riding a shopping cart down a pedestrian ramp. Jennifer keeps switching radio stations, so that we come across one song at the end, find it again in its middle, then finish with it starting all over again. I tap a quiet beat against the window. Outside, I can see cars passing by, a green station wagon with two little kids riding in the way-back, grocery bags rising like corn from the passenger seat.

It is nearly dark when we arrive at the school. Steve accidentally pulls into the bus lane, which takes us around to the back of the building. "I like your school," he says. "Very bricky."

"It's got a planetarium," Larry says.

"And an enormous tractor," Steve says.

"That's a sculpture," I say. It's this horrible, rusty assemblage called *Lunar Eclipse No. 14.* There used to be a tradition to paint it white for big games, but I don't say anything.

"There used to be a tradition to paint it white for big games," Larry says.

"Really?" Steve says. "What happened?"

"Steve," Jennifer says.

"I want to hear about this tradition," Steve says.

"Nothing happened," I say. "It just got boring."

"Boring," Steve says.

But Larry explains the whole thing, how the sculpture used to be out front, how it got moved to the middle school, then came back, only to be exiled to the back parking lot, where buses block it from view. Larry wrote an article about it for the school paper that never ran.

"We need to go," Jennifer says.

"We should bring the tradition back," Steve says, and of course Larry gets all excited. We could! He even knows where we can get some paint. He saw some inside the concession stand. Maybe it's unlocked!

"Of course its locked," I say. "Don't be dumb."

"Pull around front," Jennifer says. "Now."

Steve taps his fingers atop the steering wheel. "Let's ponder this for a moment," he says.

Never mind that the game starts in just over an hour. Never mind that cars are already pulling into the front lot. Never mind that the teams are warming up on the practice field. Never mind that Larry and I need to get our cymbals and line up in parade formation at least twenty minutes before kickoff. Never mind that Jennifer has sworn that the moment we step from the car she's going to pull away, there I am following Steve and Larry to the concession stand, my shoelaces coming untied. We're not even across the bus lane before Jennifer pulls away, middle finger raised. Steve looks at us, then shrugs. "She'll be back," he says.

We arrive at the concession stand, where two women are wiping the counter with damp rags. One wears a black hairnet, the other a green visor. A hot dog carousel turns beside them, empty. "We're not open yet, fellas," Hairnet says.

Larry puts his hands on the counter, like a little kid stepping up to a carnival game. "We're looking for paint," he says.

"Paint?" Visor says.

"It's kinda for the game," Steve says.

The two women give each other a look, then Hairnet says, "Aren't you a little old for this?"

"I'm from Red Bluff, Montana," Steve says, "and a fierce traditionalist."

"We don't have any paint," Hairnet says.

"Nachos, at half-time," Visor says.

Larry asks if we can just check around, oh please. It will just take a second.

"I don't understand half of what people find funny anymore," Hairnet says. "I really don't."

But she lets us in the back entrance, where boxes of potato chips lean from metal shelving, mops with sheepdog heads rest against an industrial sink, its faucet scarved with rags. I follow Steve. He opens cabinets, checks under the sink. Larry pulls boxes from a high shelf.

"There's nothing here," I say.

"Save the loss of tradition," Steve says.

"I didn't know cheese came in boxes," Larry says.

It's like that for a while, until Steve says, "Gentlemen, I've found it." But what he's found isn't paint, it's a white banner stuffed into a garbage can. He begins pulling it from the can, the banner unfurling like a magician's scarf. "Tonight, gentlemen, the tradition returns."

But the banner barely covers the sculpture. I watch as Steve tries wrapping it, Maypole-like, while Larry holds the loose end, already flapping hopelessly in the breeze.

"We need to go," I tell Larry. But Larry isn't listening. "Duct tape," he says. "It'd work with duct tape."

Already I can hear the percussion section warming up in the front parking lot. The trumpets running through "Hey Jude" at double speed. Clarinets clearing their slender, ducky throats.

"We'll be late," I say.

"Try poking it onto one of those pointy things," Larry says.

"Like this?" Steve says. "Aha, success! Consider yourself hereby impaled."

"Success!" Larry says, a word I've never heard him use before. When he's around his dad, he sometimes let a "neat-o" slide by.

Steve manages to drape the banner around the sculpture. "Not bad," he says. "Not perfect, but not bad either. You couldn't say it's bad." Larry agrees. He thinks it looks like a snow globe. Or a crumpled glove, he says. Steve and Larry talk about baseball gloves.

"I'm leaving," I say. I turn and start up the hill to the front parking lot. I don't even wait for Larry to say hold on or I'll be there in a second. I'm nearly running. Soon I can see the parking lot lights, casting the rest of the school into shadows.

I can almost see the band when I hear the drum major call us to attention.

Band! Ten-hut!

Hut! I say, to the darkened school. The sound of my voice makes me feel suddenly alone. I can hear it echo off the windows and walls, and I get this idea that when I turn the corner the band won't be there at all. Just a parking lot full of discarded instruments, dropped batons, a raven costume heaped onto the curb. And maybe that's why I turn back and race down the hill, looking for Larry. He's already on his way, close enough for me to shout *Hurry up,* but I don't. Instead I say what I want to say, which is *They're gone.*

THE SUMMER HE
WAS SEVEN

The summer he was seven his parents split—crr*ack*, like that—and a bird moved into the chimney. What do birds know?

One night during the summer he was seven the boy found his mother kissing the wooden banister that swirled to a point at the foot of the stairs. She had her knees in the carpet, eyes closed, hands around the bottom post like it was a man's neck. Her lips made kissy-kissy noises against the wood. The summer he was seven the lawn grew past his knees.

—

The best show during the summer he was seven was *The Price Is Right*, in which the host, Bob Barker, sometimes let the contestants hold his microphone while he took a practice putt for a game called "Hole-in-One." Although Bob Barker never won, he always sank the putt. He did not win because he was not the contestant, although the contestant often did not win because he was not Bob Barker. A contestant who was not Bob Barker but sank the putt might advance to the "Showcase Showdown."

—

The summer he was seven the air conditioning broke. Whoo-ah-whumpf, it said.

—

The boy's father visited on weekends. He took him places they'd never been before—a vineyard, a science museum, a park with nature trails—because taking him places he'd never been would remind him of how much things were still the same. At the vineyard the boy learned that thick-skinned grapes were preferable to thin-skinned grapes because thick skin kept in better flavors, although the thin-skinned ones tasted sweeter and were less sour. At the science museum the boy learned that liquid sucked through a straw was not actually "sucked" by the person sucking; rather, the liquid rose because the pressure inside the person's mouth was less than the pressure bearing down on the liquid. Few people were on the nature trails because the trails were not actually a part of nature.

—

Sometimes during the summer he was seven the boy saw the chimney bird perched atop the roof. It had black, oily feathers, and its head moved this-way-that-way-this, like every cloud was calling its name. Although appearing to be made of cotton or snow, clouds were really nothing inside. The summer he was seven the boy and his mother flew to New York.

—

"I want you to know that it's OK if you feel like you hate me sometimes," the boy's father said. They were sitting inside an empty theater, waiting for a movie to begin. "I don't want you to think that there's anything wrong with that." The boy sucked on a fat red straw, saddened by the Dr. Pepper rising to his lips, fooled, tricked, too dumb to know. "The worst thing would be to keep everything inside." The boy could see himself inside his father's glasses. "That's something your mother and I did too much, keep things inside." The summer he was seven he saw fourteen movies.

—

"There's nothing here for me now," Luke Skywalker said. "I want to learn the ways of the Force and become a Jedi like my father."

—

When his mother had kissed the banister, she'd mumbled *lovelovelove.*

—

The boy's best friend during the summer he was seven was Paul Marks. Paul went away to camp in June and came back tan. Other things were darker, too. His voice was deep and incorrect. He laughed at jokes that the boy knew Paul didn't really think were funny. "Man, I had so many girlfriends at camp," he said, as the two of them sat together in front of the television. "It's like, that's all I wanna do anymore." They were playing a video game where a slow, red plane (the boy) chased three, swift, green planes (Paul) through the sky.

—

Sometimes, on *The Price Is Right,* a contestant would bid one dollar on an item that cost thousands and end up beating the contestants who had bid thousands.

—

But why the trip to New York? They had never been a family for paintings (nudes terrified the boy), fine foods (squid confused his teeth), idle shopping (sharp pins studded the dressing room floor), or sightseeing (at the World Trade Center he'd had to venture inside the women's bathroom, all creamy tile and teasing light, when his mother didn't return; behind an unlocked stall, her sobs, as surprising and unmistakable as a middle name). Sometimes, during the summer he was seven, his electric fan spoke to him at night.

His father still loved his mother and his mother still loved his father. He still loved his parents and his parents still loved him. If a bee lands on you it is best to keep still. At his father's new apartment, the bedroom and kitchen were in the same room, although you couldn't sleep in the kitchen or eat in the bedroom. A chair is a chair and a table is a table. (But you can eat off a chair and sit on a table?)

The day they walked the nature trail, a black dog followed behind, nosing fallen leaves, twigs, growling at the dampness underneath. His fur was matted and coarse, pocked with briars and gray stems. When the boy and his father reached a narrow footbridge, the dog paraded on top, barking, daring them to cross. The boy hid behind his father's leg.

"It's okay," his father said. "He's just talking."

The boy could see the dog's black gums, and pink, jangly tongue, pulsing like a threat. "Let's go back," he said. "The other way."

His father knelt beside him. "Close one eye," he said. "Close one eye and look at the dog."

The boy obeyed.

"Now close your other eye and try switching back and forth."

The boy did this, noticing how the dog moved slightly down and to the left when he closed one eye, then back up and to the right when he closed the other.

"What happens?"

"He moves," the boy whispered, thinking *My father is showing me something. When a father shows a son something that is something.*

"So where *is* the dog? Is he where your left eye sees him, or the right?"

The boy considered this. Sometimes, before the summer he was seven, his father oiled the hinges on the bedroom doors. —, the hinges said.

"I don't know." He closed one eye and then the other.

"Maybe," his father said. "He's neither."

The summer he was seven doorknobs were not where doorknobs used to be. Paper towels, fixed between a plastic mount, wandered anyway. His toothbrush darted to the left and right of the toothbrush approximating the one between his fingers. Pop flies wavered, seeking malice. The night he watched his mother kissing the banister, he alternated closing his eyes, making her jump, dance.

———

One night the fan asked, But why are you so dirty?
Because I stopped taking baths.
Why?
Because no one tells me to anymore.
Oh.

———

They'd gotten lost in New York. How had that happened? It was dark out, he remembered that. The halos of streetlights. Store windows lit like museum displays. But city light, he discovered, was broken; there was no comfort in it. The absence settled upon him, heavily, like a dentist's bib. He sunk to the curb and put his head in his hands. "We're lost," he said. "We're lost in New York." He began to cry.

Behind him, in a dim restaurant window, dead birds suspended from white strings, their legs bound, tied.

His mother sat next to him. "Oh, it's true," she said.

A man dressed in bread bags staggered by. He had bags stuffed under his baseball cap, stretched across his face, an open slit for eyes and mouth, like a mask.

The boy hugged his arms to his chest. "We're lost in New York!" he cried, "and we'll never get home!"

His mother burst into tears. "You're right," she said. "We're lost in New York! And we'll never get home!"

——

Because the air conditioner did not work, the summer he was seven he slept with wet-combed hair, beads of water catching in his eyebrows and in the folds of his waxy ears. Although not a bath, it was like a bath.

Not really, the fan said.

——

The second-best show during the summer he was seven was M*A*S*H, where Hawkeye Pierce and his friends were in the army, but were not brave, wore flowered shirts, but were not on vacation, and played jokes on Major Frank Burns, who was silly because he longed to be brave and did not wear a flowered shirt. One time Hawkeye filled Frank's air-raid bunker with water and tricked Frank into jumping into it, which was funny because Frank thought people were trying to kill him when really they were only trying to humiliate him.

——

One night the boy slept over at Paul's house, pleased by the sound of Paul's breathing, but saddened by the indifference of the sheets balled into his hands. A digital clock marked time beside them, although the clock did not actually know what time it was. Ha, it said.

Morning: the boy slipped out of bed and went downstairs, where the early light caught in places around the family room, in the corners of the smoked glass coffee table, and across the wide, bulbous front of the television. The boy knelt before the screen and put his finger to the skin of dust there. PAUL? he wrote, in high, arching letters. When the sun angled away, the word vanished. The summer he was seven notions raged in dust.

———

Sometimes the boy opened the fireplace door, looking for the bird. He could hear the sound of its wingbeats, tiny and persistent as a pen clicking. He heard chirping. He heard cheeping. He heard bird. But where was it? He put his hand to the top of the fireplace and knocked.

Knock, knock, he said.

Click-click, said the bird.

He found a little hidden knob and wriggled it back and forth.

Clickety-click! said the bird.

When he removed his hand, it was covered with soot. Between his fingers, a long, yellow twig, curled at one end.

———

But why not take a bath? the fan asked.

He took a bath.

The water was warm and right-feeling, but the sight of his own nakedness depressed him. Dirt rose to the surface, an embarrassing thing. He rubbed the spaces between his toes and more dirt loosed itself from his body, knots of hair and flakes of skin. He stood from the tub, watching it all swirl away. The summer he was seven, he left his skin behind.

When his mother saw him toweling his hair, she said, "It's OK if you hate me."

———

If you didn't like your first Showcase, you could always pass it to the other contestant. The other contestant could not pass it back. The other contestant had to bid (without overbidding) on a grand piano, a trip to Mexico, and bumper pool. The first contestant always passed on bumper pool. Bumper pool was not the point of *The Price Is Right*. The point of *The Price Is Right* was to hear a voice announce "a *new car!*"

—

The night they were lost, a restaurant owner took them in. He served them a kind of soup that had a cloud in the middle (it wasn't a cloud) and little white dice at the bottom (no), then brought out a plate of fried carrots, broccoli, mushrooms, and shrimp that the boy and his mother dipped in a dark brown sauce. The lightness of the batter and the juiciness of the shrimp reminded the boy that he knew little of the world.

All around them, Christmas lights dangled from wires, too many for any season. Their blinks were a kind of code the boy could not crack.

"Good?" the owner asked.

"It's wonderful," the mother said.

"Very fresh, right?"

"Yes."

The boy saw the lights bloom inside his water glass.

The summer he was seven, there were other kinds of holidays.

—

But how high can grass grow?

Very, the grass said.

The boy started the mower—this was harder than he imagined—and mowed around the base of the mailbox.

That's unpleasant, the grass said.

There was a trick to mowing overgrown grass, the boy discovered: backtracking. Inching forward, listening for the near choke of the engine, then waiting for the blades to recover.

In this manner the boy mowed the lawn. It was hot out, but he did not attempt to fan himself, since the action of fanning actually makes you hotter than you were originally. A lawn mowed in three days looks no different than a lawn mowed in one evening, although these are completely different propositions.

—

The summer he was seven drew to a close.

His father said, "In so many ways, you're the smartest person I know."

His mother said, "I wonder if there will ever be a time when you see us as just plain *people*."

Paul said, "Girls hate guys with dirty ears."

Bob Barker said, "This is Bob Barker reminding you to have your pet spayed or neutered."

Hawkeye Pierce said, "I will carry on, carry over, carry a tune, Cary Grant—even hara-kiri—but I will not carry a gun."

Luke Skywalker said, "Well, take care of yourself, Han. But I guess that's what you're best at, isn't it?"

The electric fan said, But don't you feel better now?

Paul's clock said, Guess.

The air conditioner said, Whug.

The grass said, Ow.

That winter he found the bird's nest inside the fireplace. It had fallen to the iron grating, crushed to one side, twigs loose, ruined. Inside, a knot of black feathers. The boy took one and understood. *This is the way things leave.*

THE FALL OF ROME

He shouldn't have worn sneakers. That was a mistake. A shower would have helped, too. Why could he never remember that skipping a shower didn't lend him a feeling of rebelliousness, as his mirror would like to have him think, but only made him feel slimy, insecure? Conner stopped to retie his shoelace in front of the library. The library was closed now, as were the dining halls, the student center, and the university bookstore; a week ago Conner had sold back his books for Professor Palma's course, Ancient Rome. Forty-one dollars and ninety-three cents. Conner felt guilty for selling these, and had kept *The Twelve Caesars* by way of apology. He'd imagined Professor Palma watching him from a hidden window, nodding.

The campus in summer had always pleased Conner. He walked through rose gardens watered, dusted, and weeded only for him, it seemed; across the quad, where Frisbees no longer sailed; through the memorial tower archway, whose marble crest Conner had never taken the time to read—it was a luxury that he could now, if he wanted to. If he wanted to, he could do just about anything. Conner stepped out of the way to let a grounds crew pass.

When he entered Professor Palma's office, the professor greeted him by saying, "Looks like you've been shorn."

"Shorn?"

"Your hair." Professor Palma gestured Conner to a leather chair. Conner sunk into it, so that his eyes were barely level with Palma's desk. "You've cut off your long hair."

"Oh," Conner said. He hadn't cut his hair. It was odd, seeing Professor Palma seated behind a desk. Conner had never noticed, until now, how mottled his beard was. Up close, you could see patches of red, brown, blond.

"My mother always used to call that a summer cut. Every June she'd take me and my brother to the barbershop. They'd put a wooden board across the chair, to make us higher. Afterward, we'd get to pick a prize out of a plastic barrel. It was called 'Joe's Secret Barrel.' How do you like that? Joe's Secret Barrel."

"Joe's Secret Barrel," Conner said. "Well." He felt himself smiling his nervous smile.

"Comic books, mostly. And bubble gum. Bazooka Joe."

What would happen, Conner wondered, if he never got around to asking his question? "Professor Palma," he said. "I have a small problem I'd like to bring to your attention."

Professor Palma nodded. "I see." In class, Professor Palma sometimes steepled his hands across his face in the middle of lectures. "Ladies and gentlemen of the jury," he'd say, "let me submit the following."

"It's about my final grade," Conner said. "You gave me a B-minus, which I totally understand, because of the midterm and everything, but the thing is—" Conner suddenly had no idea how he was to finish the sentence. How did anyone know how to finish their sentences? Professor Palma was looking at him like he was explaining how to butter toast. "The thing is, I was wondering if there was any way you could change it to a B-plus."

Professor Palma drew his lips together and nodded. "I see."

"I'm really sorry to ask," Conner said. "I know how annoying grade change requests can be. That's why I didn't e-mail you about it. I thought a meeting would be better." He offered a clumsy smile.

"A meeting," Professor Palma said.

"Right."

"Face to face. Mano y mano." Professor Palma chopped the air with his hand.

Conner nodded. Behind Professor Palma, he noticed a bulletin board crammed with postcards, cartoons, photographs. In the largest photograph, Professor Palma standing atop a windy mountain, a woman beside him, a little girl in a pink baseball cap clutching Professor Palma's leg.

"I'm not quite sure where to begin," Professor Palma said.

"I'm sorry," Conner said. "I'm only asking because I think my participation toward the end of the semester really picked up and I didn't miss a class all year and," Conner felt himself losing some sort of advantage, "and if I get a B-plus I'll be able to go to the honors graduation ceremony next year." Why did he always say more than he wished? He felt his face grow warm. "My parents are coming," he added, idiotically.

"Well, that's quite a lot for us to think about, isn't it?"

"Yes."

Professor Palma next addressed his fingers, which were quite large, Conner noticed. "Please know that I'm not in the habit of giving grade changes, although my students seem to be forever in the habit of asking for them."

"I know."

"Students seem to think that a grade is something negotiable. I'm not sure why this is," Professor Palma said, then raised one eyebrow, "but I have my theories."

Conner, expecting one, was surprised when the professor only opened his desk drawer and rummaged through. The open drawer gave off a smell of chalk dust and damp wood. "As I was saying, I have my theories. A part of me wonders if the feeling of negotiability arises from a student's sense of entitlement, a problem I've wrestled with all my academic life, but more in recent years. I sometimes wonder if there's a new breed of student on the rise, quick and on the make, philosophically opposed to failure, but morally blind to failure's lessons. Do you see what I mean?"

"Mmm."

"And another part of me wonders if, as students evolve, as a university certainly hopes they will, their thinking evolves, too, and, attendant to this growth—I think of it as peeking over a high fence, for some reason—is the slow realization that all grades, as all knowledge perhaps is, are inherently subjective. Am I right? That question of 'What really is the difference between a B-minus and a B-plus,' or that nagging question 'What are the clear, defensible, and unalterable criteria for an A?'"

"Right." The flesh around Professor Palma's eyes nurtured a single brown mole. "I see what you're saying, but it's more that—"

"The Unanswerable Question!" Professor Palma laughed, as if this had been a joke between them all along.

"Right."

Outside, two pigeons landed on the sill of Professor Palma's window. They made a noise like liquid pouring into tall glasses.

"I wouldn't ask. Normally, I mean."

"My wife says I have too many theories about things. A little secret for you to remember: no one knows you better than your wife."

"Right."

Professor Palma looked at his watch. "I'm sorry, but I'm meeting someone else at noon."

"I'm sorry to ask for this," Conner said. "I really am. But I'm not asking because I think an exception should be made for me." He tried to read Professor Palma's expression, but the expression conveyed only imperfect vision, cloudy skies, and a single, unasked question: was it Colin or Conan? "I'm just asking because I think I've earned it."

"Well, I'm sympathetic," Professor Palma said, "to a point. But you most certainly are asking that an exception be made for you. That's without debate." He continued before Conner could point out that one of the pigeons had now made its way inside the office and was currently bobbing toward the glinty magnifying glass atop Professor Palma's *Oxford English Dictionary*. "But I suppose that's the human condition, isn't it? Thinking an exception will be made for us. Hoping the universe is Godded indeed, and hears our call."

As if a punchline, the phone rang.

"Excuse me." Professor Palma picked up the receiver. "Yes, speaking," he said. "The Camry. Right. Yes, I spoke to Henry about that. I said I spoke to Henry about that. Right." The pigeon, forgetting the object of its desire, was now sitting just inside the window. It looked at Conner without really looking at him, somehow. Eyes like shrunken pennies. "That's not what Henry said at all." The professor shook his head. Was the change of grade form in his desk? Conner wondered. "Well, you'll have to let me talk to Henry about that," Professor Palma said. "I said you'll have to have to let me talk to Henry about that. Right. Fine. Yes, that's my home number. Right." He hung up. "Mechanics," he sighed. "But of what?"

"Professor," Conner said.

Professor Palma checked his watch again, then pulled a carbon ledger from the desk drawer. "I will keep this with me, Conner," he said, "as a reminder of our meeting." He filled in a few lines, then folded it in half. "I will keep this with me and think about our meeting."

Conner felt the advantage swing his way, like a hurled rope. How could he mention that the form needed to be submitted by tomorrow? "Thanks," Conner said. "There's just one more little thing. It seems that the deadline—"

At that moment, Professor Palma's door flew open. A beautiful, impossibly skinny woman entered the room and immediately began swatting the pigeons away with a rolled-up newspaper. "Dirty, filthy birds!" she cried. She knocked into Conner's chair. "Why do you let them do this, Gerald? Why?"

"Calm down, Magda," Professor Palma said. "Please."

Magda closed the dictionary with a sudden, thunderous clap. "Making filth on these beautiful books. Please to go! Go!" She chased one pigeon out the window, then cornered the other near Professor Palma's bookcase. The pigeon bobbed its head and spread its ugly wings. For a moment Conner was afraid the pigeon was going to fly around the room, but then Magda unrolled the newspaper like an enormous catcher's mitt and, with one, startling motion, scooped the bird up and deposited it out the window. "There!" she said. She pushed the window down, which screeched to a close. "Filthy bird."

It would be hard to say that anyone looked attractive scooping a live pigeon into a newspaper, so how had this woman managed to do so? Perhaps it was the breath heaving in her chest, or the way she now brushed her gorgeous, silky hair—it really was silky—from her eyes without the least trace of self-consciousness. Maybe it was the clothes she wore, a white halter top and strangely dark, European-looking jeans, cut low enough to expose her brown stomach, with its taut belly button like a punctuation mark. But more likely it was because Conner had been in love with this mysterious woman all semester. Magda. This woman who sat in the front row, challenging Professor Palma with her sharp, angry questions, flipping the pages of her exotic notebook with a barely contained rage, crossing and recrossing her long legs from which expensive-looking, high-heeled shoes dangled, even on snowy days. His friends had a name for her, one of Conner's inventions. *Frenchy.*

"Do you know Magda?" Professor Palma said. "Magda, this is—."

"Conner," Conner said. He shook her hand, which had rings on every finger.

"Magda is helping me on a dig this summer," Professor Palma said. "In lovely Tunisia." He laughed like this, too, was some sort of joke.

"Oh," Conner said.

"These filthy birds, I hate them. Why do you let them have their way, Gerald?"

Professor Palma made a *beats me?* face. "I suppose I'm too soft," he said.

Magda made a tsk noise, then pulled a spool of tape from her purse and tossed it onto Professor Palma's desk. "This won't work," she said. "They fall down." She removed a bundle of yellow flyers, half-sheets of paper bound with a rubber band. "Please try something else."

"Magda is helping me look for volunteers for the dig," Professor Palma explained.

"Every one, down. I go back, try again, but forget it. Down again." Magda lifted a stapler from Professor Palma's desk. "Maybe this," she said. She tried stuffing the stapler in her purse, but it wouldn't fit.

"I was just telling Conner that I was on my way to another meeting," Professor Palma said. "With Dr. Ancusi."

Magda threw her hands up in the air. "*Why?* We're never going to get out of here. Already it's—" she checked her watch. "Please, come on, Gerald."

The rope that had once swung so close now made a second appeal. "I could help," Conner offered. "I mean, with the flyers. It's no problem."

Professor Palma looked not at him, but at Magda. "Sounds like you've found a volunteer," he said.

Magda sighed. "Fine," she said. "If this is how you do it, Gerald." She handed Conner the stapler. "But we're leaving soon, right? I'm so hungry."

"Right," Professor Palma said. "We'll meet back here in fifty-five minutes or so."

"Fifty-five minutes or so," Magda said. "You American men. Can't even say 'an hour' without covering your tracks."

When they were about to leave, Professor Palma glanced at Conner and said, "I'll be thinking about our meeting."

———

Outside it was getting cloudy. It would be a rainy day after all. How had Conner not noticed the saplings along the college mall offering up their silvery undersides like raised pom-poms? Clouds gathered above the administration building, blanching the gold from its dome. He and Magda walked along the mall, where work crews were repairing the pedestrian walkway, whose intricate brickwork had always secretly pleased Conner. He liked it that the university lavished so much attention on his walk home, to the dining hall, to the classrooms where he was so often a star.

"Already they fall apart," Magda said. She kicked a small stone a remarkable distance. "A quarter million dollars, for what?"

"Yeah," Conner said. "It's crazy." He had already given up on flirting, from the moment Magda descended the history department stairs in twos and threes, leaving him to his hurried but cautious single steps behind her. But maybe he'd given up too soon. Although it was growing darker, Magda donned a pair of enormous, yellow sunglasses.

"This whole place is crazy," she said. "Look!" She pointed to the workmen walking the scaffolding outside the geology building. "The whole place falls down. They throw money away on nothing!"

Conner nodded. Listening to Magda, with her waving

arms and mirrored lenses, was like being scolded by a gorgeous, fantastic insect. "I know," he said. "This place drives me crazy."

They separated to place flyers on the notice boards flanking the walkway entrance. The boards were freckled with concert notices, sublet announcements, weeks out of date. It saddened Conner to think of the old notices; he didn't like their suggestion of empty apartments, darkened stages, of good times long gone. He stapled Professor Palma's flyers atop posters for free condoms. *Want To Earn $$$ AND Discover The World?* the flyers began. Conner couldn't imagine Professor Palma thinking up the dollar signs. Maybe those were Magda's idea.

She returned to him now and began her conversation again as if no time had passed whatsoever. "They throw away what is worth keeping and keep everything that is junk. Junk!" She ran ahead to the next board and stapled three flyers in the time it took Conner to staple one. "This is a junk place, right? Just look around. Tell me this isn't!" Before Conner could answer, Magda grabbed a handful of his flyers and began stapling them to a large tree.

"Uh, I don't think you're supposed to do that," Conner said.

Magda turned an angry look on him. "Why?" She punctuated her question with a punch of the stapler. "Why should we care when they don't? Tell me why."

"Well—" Do not say, Because I like these trees. "Because I don't think that's what Professor Palma wants."

"Ha!" Magda said. She ran ahead to the next tree and stapled another flyer. "There! That's what Professor Palma wants."

Conner, sensing whatever chances of gaining Magda's interest he might have had slipping beyond his reach, grabbed one of the tree flyers and tore it in half. "I don't think so," he said. He stuffed the torn flyer into his pocket.

Magda looked at him with what seemed new respect, he thought. "Ha!" she said, then raced to another tree, stapling two flyers at once.

"Not the trees," Conner said. He tore the flyers down, but Magda only laughed and darted across the quad, where a grounds crew was distributing mulch beneath a bronze statue of Thomas Jefferson. The Jefferson Garden was intended to make Jefferson look deep in pastoral contemplation, but somehow conveyed the sense that he was horribly lost and preposterously overdressed, a wedding guest wandering from a wrecked car. When Magda passed the crew, the three crew members stopped working, gawked. "I'd run, too, boy!" one of them called to Conner. Conner turned to acknowledge him, but only caught Jefferson's bronzed gaze.

"You have very high morals," Magda said when Conner reached her. She swiped the rest of Conner's flyers from his hands. "You are a moral person, right?" She laughed, then stapled a clumsy row of flyers along a low tree branch. "A good boy."

Conner was about to contradict her, when the clouds opened up and rain began to fall. He pulled the flyers from the branch. "It's starting to rain," he said.

"But not on you," Magda laughed. She kept stapling the branch, testing him. "Not on the perfect student."

I'm not the perfect student, Conner wanted to say, but, in a way, he was. He had a high grade point average, arrived early to every class, pledged the best fraternity, volunteered to lead blood drives, food donations, Toys for Tots. *Would you like to lead this class?* one professor had written across the bottom of his essay exam. *Let me know when you need a letter of recommendation—please!* But, for all his other successes, Conner had failed to gain Professor Palma's admiration. Every day, he'd sat in the front row, taking copious notes, raising his hand to nearly every question. He'd memorized whole passages from Suetonius, and occasionally worked these into his responses, hoping Professor Palma would recognize them, but Professor

Palma only nodded, dismissing him. "Yes, well, there's that, of course," he'd say, then call on someone else, his gaze passing over Conner like a swift cloud. When Magda spoke, Professor Palma nodded enthusiastically, said, "Yes, right. Good observation," or, most aggravating to Conner, "That's perfectly said." Each week Conner kept a private count of who had raised their hand more often, him or Magda, making sure to keep ahead. Now, he watched her staple another flyer to a sapling still tied by ropes, and wondered if she and Professor Palma were sleeping together.

"We should get out of this rain," Conner said.

Magda ignored him. "Who cares if it rains?" she said.

"Well, I'm going back."

Magda turned to face him, revealing, for the first time, the outline of her breasts through her rain-soaked shirt. She smiled a crooked smile. "So, go back, then," she said. There were tiny beads of rain on her sunglasses, like jewels. It began to pour.

Conner was deciding whether he really wanted to leave or not—what did that smile mean?—when Magda broke into a sprint and ran to the Jefferson statue, from which the grounds crew had since fled. Conner followed her without trying to appear to. Magda was eyeing the Jefferson statue for a likely staple spot, when she took one flyer and punched it over Jefferson's bronze quill. The flyer sagged in the rain, but Magda had places for others: the points of Jefferson's three corner hat, his pondering finger, raised, as if asking a question, even, against all physics, the tip of his nose. Conner stood behind her, watching her handiwork. Then he stepped closer and found himself touching her shoulder, her damp, exciting shoulder. "Magda," he said. But Magda sped away, laughing. Conner followed.

"You made him into a clown," Conner said, when he reached her under the memorial tower archway. He wanted his tone to be conspiratorial, but it came out as an accusation. He could not catch his breath. Magda was watching the rain, her arms hugged to her chest. She shrugged. "This place makes lots of clowns." They stood that way for a while, not talking. Conner wondered whether he'd done the right thing, touching her, then felt angry at himself for worrying about that. Why wouldn't Magda face him?

"Do you know they want to get rid of Professor Palma?" Magda said.

"They do?"

Magda nodded. "They say they want him to retire, but they just want him out."

"Oh."

"But Gerald wants to stay. He wants to stay, but they want him to leave." Magda made a noise that Conner thought might mean tears, but when Magda faced him, she was not crying. "It's crazy. Even his wife—his own wife!—wants him to leave. Can you believe it? For what? So she can play golf and drive a big car. Gerald would die living that way. Can you see him playing golf?"

Conner could very well see him playing golf—he was surprised he didn't already, actually—but shook his head no.

"No," Magda said. "But his wife—" she waved her hand. "Don't let's talk about her."

Conner stepped close enough that he could see the goose-flesh of Magda's damp arms. A thin bracelet clung to her wrist, made entirely of string. In class, she sometimes pared a large apple with a small knife while Conner watched, the lecture a sudden jumble of slides and maps, Professor Palma's voice a radio from a passing car. "I'm sorry," Conner said.

"For what?" Magda said, then began to cry. When Conner placed a hand on her shoulder, Magda pushed it aside. "You shouldn't pay attention to a woman's tears," she said. She walked to the other side of the archway, peering out at the rain falling across the quad. At times, the rain blew in from the archway, but Magda did not move to the middle, where Conner stood, wondering if he should approach her again.

"I'm so hungry," Magda said, to no one in particular.

"Yeah," Conner said. Once, he'd followed Magda after

class. Just for a few moments, until she turned toward south campus, walking against the traffic lights, her notebook clutched beneath her arm. Conner stopped at the light, feeling suddenly ridiculous and creepy. What was he doing?

"I'm so sick of this," Magda said, but Conner couldn't tell if she meant the rain or university or something else altogether. But he knew one thing, and it was a surprise to him: he was about to approach Magda and put his arms around her, gently, if she would have him. If she would have him, he would lean in for a kiss.

"I'm so sick of waiting," Magda said. She wiped her eyes. "I really am." And, before Conner could reach her, she was off running again, through the rain and across the quad, puddles exploding from her feet. Conner hesitated, then followed. Thank God, he thought, as he reached the history department, where the door was still flung open wide, rain blowing in. Thank God I didn't.

———

Conner found them in Professor Palma's office, Professor Palma donning an enormous raincoat thirty years out of style. Magda was behind him, looping a thick belt through the coat, straightening the shoulders.

"Rain gear," Professor Palma said. "Ah, who knows the caprices of the weather?"

"Please keep still," Magda said. She reached the belt around him, then tightened it in the front. "You move it's not going to work."

"I'm under strict orders, as you can see," Professor Palma said. He had his arms raised like a child.

"I see," Conner said.

"I was just telling Magda, as it turns out I didn't have a meeting at all," Professor Palma said. "I had my days mixed up."

Magda clicked her tongue. "You get everything mixed up, Gerald."

"I make no argument. Guilty as charged," Professor Palma laughed. Conner offered a weak smile. How good it would feel to leave this office. How good it would be to leave this campus. Why had he come here in the first place? "But I'll have you know I made a nice hour of it, listening to the rain and catching up on my reading. It's a fortunate day when I can find the time to catch up on my reading."

Conner was about to mention the deadline for the grade change, when Magda pulled a floppy rain hat down over Professor Palma's ears. "There," she said.

"Well," Professor Palma said, "as you can see, it looks like we're about to depart." Magda placed a folded umbrella in his hand. "Whose is this?" he asked.

"Yours," Magda said. "Let's go, Gerald. I'm so hungry."

"We're going to eat," Professor Palma said, "but I'll be thinking about our meeting, won't I, Colin?"

"Thanks," Conner said.

"Gerald," Magda said. She tugged his sleeve.

"You can leave the rest of the flyers on my desk," Professor Palma said. "I hope I can trust you to close the door behind you until it clicks, if you don't mind. We seem to be having a small food emergency here."

Magda pulled Professor Palma out the door. "Oh, he's very trustworthy," she said. "He's got high morals."

Professor Palma seemed not to hear. He gave one last look at Conner, his smiling head pinched between the folds of his rain hat, a look that conveyed how happy he was to be bundled in his coat, a meal on the way, the pleasure he took in being someone who could be looked after and adored, whose most minor requests were matters of consequence, someone who, despite all his years, still mattered, who deeply, deeply mattered. "Until it clicks," he said.

Conner stood in the office until he could no longer hear their footsteps. The rain beat against the windowpanes, closed now. He placed the flyers on the desk and was about to leave the office when he saw a solitary piece of paper in the trash can. The grade change form, still folded in the middle. Conner unfolded it to find that Professor Palma hadn't filled in a thing, except, absurdly, his signature at the bottom. The signature was oversized, nearly illegible. Conner folded the form into his pocket.

And it wasn't his walk across the rainy campus that perplexed Conner, nor was handing the slip to the woman at the registrar's office, who barely read it over while chewing a pen, nor was it the ease with which he'd found himself saying, "It's an A," when she asked what grade to enter—none of these things troubled Conner on his walk home. Only this: why, with all the rain shading them from the world, with its sudden loan of permission, why hadn't he the courage to kiss Magda?

THE FRENCH GIRLS

When the French girls came, I was halfway through *Lord of the Flies*. When the French girls came, my two best friends were Jonathan Akers and Matt Drew. Jonathan had a head shaped like a flipped pail and sometimes wore his raincoat to class, where he made a show of removing a gold Cross pen from its inner pocket, then testing its tip against his tongue. He was fond of Pringles. We sometimes spent the weekend at Matt's house, where his mother allowed us to swim late into the night in their heated pool, the pool lights sending fantastic paisley shapes onto the underside of trees, making the sound of our voices feel strangely intimate and incorrect, like tourists in a cathedral. When the French girls came, my hands smelled of chlorine.

There were three of them: Broomstick, Eyebrows, and Phoebe Cates. Part of some unlucky cultural exchange, they materialized in early autumn and stayed until homecoming, where they politely refused to ride a float fitted out with papier-mâché tigers roasting helmeted eagles over an open flame. In Mr. Hansen's history class, they fell asleep during a filmstrip about the Hindenburg. They ate nothing—nothing, not one thing—from their lunch trays. They nearly smoked cigarettes in the planetarium until Mrs. Debrosky turned her laser pointer on them and flipped the lights. They found this funny. I know; I was sitting right behind them. When the lights went down, I put my feet on the back of Phoebe's seat and felt a kind of electricity course through my knees. When the French girls came, I was fourteen.

"I'd take Eyebrows over Phoebe," Jonathan said, hugging the rim of Matt's pool. Matt lifted himself from the deep end ladder. "No way," he said. "I'm Phoebe all the way."

"Me, too," I said, although I secretly preferred Broomstick. She would, I imagined, one day realize that I was the only one who truly understood her beauty.

"Phoebe!" Matt shouted. "You eez a hottie, no? Oui-oui!"

When the French girls came, I had never so much as hugged a girl.

Homecoming week it rained. Marching band drilled indoors, where our drum major saluted the French girls before leading us into "The Rose" which ended with the drum major collapsing—slowly, dramatically, and with great feeling—onto the gym floor. When I looked up I saw Broomstick crying with laughter.

That afternoon the French girls sat with us at lunch. "It's OK, right?" Eyebrows asked.

"Yes, OK," we said.

I ate two slices of pizza without tasting a thing. The French girls spoke as if observing a distant parade. "These are tradition?" Phoebe said, indicating the homecoming balloons nudging the ceiling.

"Sort of," Matt said.

"It's for homecoming," I said, and Eyebrows nodded.

"Homecoming," Broomstick sighed. "Ah, already I'm missing this place so much."

LIKE THAT

That a life could go many ways was no secret to Caitlin Drury; still she had a difficult time accounting for her own. She was fifty-six, divorced, and drawn to things she had little aptitude for. She took a watercolor course at a community college (she couldn't draw a stick figure), listened to Purcell at the breakfast table (the only music that made any sense to her was doo-wop), and had just enough disparate and diverse friends to effectively cancel each other out at parties. At night, the sound of a slow train passing through town filled her with a strange sense of wonder and dread.

Still, her life was not all gray. She enjoyed herself pretty well sometimes, she figured. Like sitting in the kitchen with the lights turned low, chatting on the telephone with her daughter, Alissa. Alissa lived in New York with a group of girls—*women*, she reminded herself—who were all pursuing degrees of some sort or another. She could never figure it all out exactly, but she didn't like to pry. Caitlin secretly admired her reluctance to ask too many questions about things she shouldn't. She always tried to keep her conversations cheery with her daughter, not wanting to be nosy.

"I took such a nice walk today," she said, hoping Alissa would approve. For years, her daughter had accused her of not getting enough exercise, and she had taken up walking in part to appease her. Usually she walked through the unlit streets of her neighborhood, her heart racing whenever a car slowed to pass. She would squint in the glare of the headlights, offering a wave to whoever was inside, wishing that she were riding along with them, instead of returning home to an empty house. As the car disappeared ahead, Caitlin imagined the driver looking in the rearview mirror, saying, "That Caitlin Drury is certainly getting *her* exercise."

"That's wonderful," Alissa said. "I hope you wrote about your walking experience in your journal."

"Oh, I will," Caitlin lied, trying to remember where she had placed the blank book Alissa had given her last Christmas. Once, Alissa had asked her what kind of things she wrote about in the journal and Caitlin could only think to say, "Oh, you know, addresses, recipes, that kind of thing," to which Alissa had criticized her for not writing about the right kinds of things.

"Like what?" Caitlin had asked.

"Like thoughts. Emotions. *Feelings*."

And that night, in bed, Caitlin had sat with the book propped between her knees, trying to think of the right thing to write about. *I feel lonely* she wrote, then crossed it out. She didn't like the idea of someone coming along later to read her journal, finding out she felt lonely. She crossed it out a few more times, then wrote, *It's cold out tonight. Brrr!* She drew a little face with a zigzag mouth and huge, lopsided earmuffs, then closed the book and fell into an easy sleep.

Loneliness. Well, there were cures for that, weren't there? Certainly she was not without friends (she was inwardly proud of the number of phone messages she sometimes received on a single weekend, her answering machine blinking like a poked eye) but lately she had grown tired of them. Too often Caitlin felt she was having the same conversation over and over, the discussion a single thread spooled between them, feeding out and taking up again. She sat listening to herself spew out her usual litany of worries—money, health, her secret fear of interstates—wondering why she even bothered anymore. Her friends now seemed to her too quick to comfort and console, not quite listening somehow.

"Oh, you'll never believe this," Caitlin would say, recalling a mishap in the express aisle. "But today I went to the super-market just to get a gallon of milk—"

"God, *I've* done that!" the friend would interject, laughing like it was the funniest thing they'd heard in years.

Well, she had wanted sympathy from others, hadn't she? Wasn't that, in fact, what everyone wanted from everyone else? The truth was, she didn't really know what she wanted anymore. She had wanted to be married (done), have a child (check), and ease into her middle years with a sense of satisfaction and fulfillment (OK, OK, two out of three). So what next? This was the trick of fifty-six: you were finally free to plan a new campaign, but suddenly all your maps were obsolete.

"You know," she once told Alissa, "I really feel connected to this town."

"That's good," Alissa said. "I'm glad to hear it."

And this was the truth: she really did feel connected to the town. She had retired the year before from her job at the post office—she had been the postmaster so long she could identify the handwriting of every child in her neighborhood, often writing in a return address if they had forgotten—and had felt a rare sort of citizenship within that role. Now, though, she didn't know where she stood. True, she couldn't make a simple bank deposit without three tellers asking how Alissa was doing, each leaning out of their cubicles like racehorses testing the gate. But what did that prove?

"Oh, she's good, very goood," Caitlin would say, licking the seal on the deposit envelope.

"Does she know what she's going to do after she graduates?"

"Well, she'd like to teach English," Caitlin lied, recalling the last time she'd mentioned the idea to Alissa. "Mom, I'm getting a degree in *poetry*," Alissa had said, "not diagramming sentences." "Well," Caitlin had said, "I just think you would make a wonderful teacher," trying to hide the fact that she thought being a poet was just about the silliest thing she'd ever heard. She'd been to one of Alissa's "readings," and hadn't understood a word of it, except for "fuck," which made her lower herself to the table and hide behind a pepper grinder.

"Oh, that would be nice, wouldn't it." The tellers nodded in agreement. "Is she thinking of settling around here?"

Caitlin felt the air slowly shutting off around her. "Well, she's thinking of moving back home for a while, you know, just to get her plans situated." She smiled at them, pleasantly. "She really doesn't know yet."

"Well, that will certainly be nice to have her back around the house again, at least for a little while."

Caitlin agreed that yes, it would.

Back around the house again. A door swung open inside her at the thought of it, revealing Alissa tucked inside an undersized bed, covers pulled to the floor. Caitlin imagined herself pulling the covers to Alissa's chin, then moving a comma of hair from her cheek.

"Mom," Alissa moaned, "I'm asleep."

"Does it feel funny to be in your old bed?"

Alissa buried her face in the pillow.

"Because it looks funny to see you there," Caitlin said. "Funny, good funny, I mean."

"Sure," Alissa grumbled, "it's a riot."

To have her daughter come home. She turned the idea over in her mind, slowly, letting it take hold. Usually this happened on Sunday evenings, long after the euphoria of coffee, crosswords, and public radio had worn away, and she found herself pacing around the house in bedroom slippers, speaking to herself in half-sentences.

"Well, that's OK," she said to the living room, turning off the lights by the upright piano.

"That's fine," she mumbled to the sliding glass doors, watching a steady rain fall outside. The reflection from the interior lights made it look like she was standing within and without her backyard. She could see her legs inside the patio furniture.

"Super duper," she whispered.

A cloud of breath mushroomed before her.

The rain beat against the glass.

———

The year before, Caitlin had traveled to New York to visit Alissa. It was Thanksgiving weekend, and the city exuded the smell of snow, although the sky was fair and cloudless. Caitlin met Alissa at the train station.

"Mom," Alissa said, spotting her mother's suitcase, "you're only staying for a weekend. That's two days, not twenty."

"I know how many days there are in a weekend," Caitlin said, attempting to lift the suitcase. "And, besides, who says that I'm not moving in?"

Alissa took the handle with both hands.

"That was a joke," Caitlin said.

Caitlin entered Alissa's small, cramped apartment, with its peeled paint, uneven floors, and faint odor of litter boxes. Above them, the neighbors' footsteps sounded like heavy boots tracking through wet, packed snow.

"This is such a cozy little place," Caitlin said, thinking, I'll scrub the bathroom when Alissa's asleep.

Alissa flopped herself down on the sofa. "Do you realize that's what you've said *every* time you've seen where I'm living? 'This is such a cozy little place.' God! Why is it that everything you say is a parody of everything else you've already said?"

The weekend went along in this manner. When Caitlin offered to help prepare the Thanksgiving meal—Alissa was hosting a dinner for her friends—Alissa allowed her to chop scallions, the two working side by side, silently, as water boiled on the range. "This will be my first Thanksgiving without ham or turkey," Caitlin said, hoping to draw Alissa into some pleasant chit chat. Alissa turned to rinse a head of lettuce in the sink.

"Please, don't start," she said.

For years their conversations had gone this way, shadowed by something vague and unspoken. Caitlin watched Alissa as she pressed water from the lettuce leaves, observing the way her shoulders rose in the effort. There was a tenderness there that startled her, momentarily, and she busied herself again with the scallions, slicing them into tiny swatches of green. Outside, an ambulance could be heard passing in the distance, renewing the degree of silence between them.

Alissa's friends arrived later in the evening, each bringing some sort of food—humus, sourdough bread, basmati rice—which Caitlin helped set on the table, pleased to introduce herself as Alissa's mother. For their part, the friends seemed generally unimpressed by the novelty of her visit, offering a lukewarm little "hello" or a loose, fishy handshake. Caitlin startled one of Alissa's roommates by hugging her as soon as she walked in the door, her arms nestling two overstuffed grocery bags.

"Oh, I've heard so much about you!" Caitlin said, trying to recall which roommate was the one who never remembered to deliver her messages. The roommate stared at Caitlin as if she were a flipped bus.

"I'm Alissa's mother," Caitlin explained.

Moments later the group seated themselves around the

kitchen table, sitting shoulder to shoulder as a strange silence settled upon them. Caitlin sat across from Alissa, privately marrying her to the only two male friends present, wondering if she should try a joke to loosen things up. "Well, it's sure awwfully quiet in here," she said, giving the group a cheerleader smile. "The food *must* be good!"

Alissa's friends nodded silently, their mouths full, as Alissa softly kicked her underneath the table. *Please,* she mouthed.

Such serious young people, Caitlin thought, listening in as they compared travel experiences in the Peace Corps. She was confused by the way they spoke to one another, addressing each other in the careful, restrained manner of a job interview.

"I've always found it helpful to keep a ledger of all my expenses, especially if I'm traveling with friends who may be unfamiliar with the exchange rate," one said, as the others nodded in agreement.

"Also, I try to avoid dining alone when I'm traveling by myself," another said. "Meals are such an excellent opportunity to meet fellow students and share information."

"Oh, I know what you mean," Caitlin said. "I can't eat my dinner without Peter Jennings."

They finished their desserts, quietly. Caitlin watched Alissa as she talked with the boy (man?) next to her. She watched the way her hands held the stem of a water glass— such young, pretty hands, she thought. She listened to the young talk of these young people, delighted by the presence of bodies, shoulders, voices around her. She could feel an elbow gently resting against her side, prodding her, like a sleeping puppy. And then, slowly, a dim awareness that everyone was staring at her.

"Mom," Alissa said, "you're crying."

Caitlin fumbled with her napkin, trying to unfold a corner.

"Mom, what is it?"

Caitlin buried her face in her hands.

"I'm just so happy to be here," she said.

— ◆ —

Whenever Caitlin thought of Alissa coming home, a yellow house returned itself to her imagination. The house, partially obscured by a row of poplar trees, was a misremembrance of her grandparents' home, a low, squat ranch bordered by tall hedges on two sides. It was the home Caitlin and her sister sometimes visited in the winter, when the wind rattled the windows in the evening, and the air smelled of woodsmoke.

She had been eight the last time she visited and had spent most of her time correcting her sister, Cassie, on the right way to tie a braid. Their grandparents had given them a new board game that no one could figure out, and the two sisters sat at the kitchen table while their grandfather read the directions with a magnifying glass, the game splayed before them like a battle map.

"'Each player moves two tokens from the START square, odd numbers for the red token, even numbers for the blue,'" their grandfather read, as Cassie took one of the tokens and shoved it inside her mouth.

"Lookh, Caitluhn," she said, swishing it inside her cheek, "I got uh frogh in m'mouf!"

Caitlin took a token and did the same. "Me tooh," she giggled.

And the day had become one of those ten or twenty days that, born out of boredom and glee, stamped itself upon Caitlin's mind as the happiest she had ever been. She thought about it often, when she said good-bye to Alissa on the telephone, or curled inside her bed with the reading lamp on.

What she had forgotten, though, was the ending to that day. She and Cassie had hugged their grandparents good-bye, saddened to see the day close, and zipped themselves up in their thick winter coats. Their grandfather helped them tie the hood strings.

"Hey, who's a pretty princess?" he said, tucking their hair inside.

They pulled at his shirt, begging to stay.

But it was in the car, as her parents drove away, that Caitlin realized something: she had forgotten her mittens inside. She'd left them on the countertop when she was putting on her coat. Her parents turned the car back and slowed into the driveway, the house still lit from inside, as Caitlin hopped out to retrieve the mittens. Her grandfather met her at the door.

"Did you forget these?" he said, handing her the mittens.

She took them, dumbly, and nodded.

"Well, I'll bet you'll need your mittens tonight, won't you?"

Caitlin nodded, staring past him into the kitchen. There was something shoddy about that room now, shoddy, too, in the gesture of returning the mittens. She had come and played and giggled until her sides ached and the house had gone on without her, the kitchen table wiped clean with a damp rag. She had been, she felt, forgotten.

"It's cold out tonight," her grandfather said.

Caitlin hugged herself, performing a little shiver. "Brrr," she said.

———

Caitlin was on the telephone with Alissa. "Guess who's getting married?" she said in a singsong voice. Alissa sighed. "Some fool," she replied.

Caitlin wasn't sure if this was supposed to be a joke or not, but she laughed anyway. "No, Tommy DuBois," she said.

"Christ," Alissa said. "There's a tragedy in the making."

Caitlin could never understand why her daughter had such contempt for marriage. Once, on Alissa's twentieth birthday, Caitlin had cheerily looked across the dinner table and remarked, "Just think, you're the same age I was when I married your father," to which Alissa had only responded, "Hey, that's not my problem."

Now, she listened as Alissa recounted a time she and Tommy scribbled their names on a bus seat, trying to think of the right way to invite her to the ceremony. "You know," she said, casually, "the invitation is for myself and a guest . . ." she trailed off. "Just in case you were wondering."

"Mom, I'm not going to Tommy DuBois's wedding. The whole idea of seeing everyone I hated in high school totally depresses me."

Everyone she hated in high school? What was that supposed to mean? "I'm sure everyone would love to see you," Caitlin said, hopefully. "And, who knows, maybe you'll meet someone," she said, suddenly wishing she hadn't.

"Good-bye, Mom," Alissa said, sighing. "I think we need to hang up now."

"Honey, I'm sorry," Caitlin said, "I didn't mean that."

"Well, maybe you shouldn't say things you don't really mean, then."

"You're right," Caitlin said. "You're very, very right."

She considered apologizing again, but instead discovered herself recalling a time she and Alissa rescued a baby robin from a swimming pool, its eggy eyes staring out from a slick body, heavy as a dunked donut. And, in the misplaced memory of this, she found herself saying, "I love you, Alissa."

"Mom," Alissa said.

"More than you could ever know."

A forest of silence sprang up between them, suddenly, wholly.

"Listen," Alissa said, "Maybe I'll think about going to this wedding. I'm not promising anything, though."

"No, of course not," Caitlin said, zipping her into the green dress she'd given her last Christmas.

"I'll let you know," Alissa said.

That night, Caitlin dusted the dresser in Alissa's old room, running the cloth along the top of each empty drawer.

———

The thought of Alissa returning home, if only for a weekend, was a hand upon Caitlin's shoulder. She felt it when she stopped in to see her friends at the post office, sitting with a cup of coffee between her knees as they sorted parcels into bins. She chatted happily about life after retirement, sending the others into low, appreciative whistles, as they went about their business.

"Wouldn't you know?" she said. "I've been trying to place this tune all day, and here it is on the radio." She hummed along for a moment, trying to recall the title.

It was this kind of feeling, a strange giddiness, that now informed all her conversations. Suddenly she could no longer pay attention to what anyone said while eating a meal. She sat inside a sandwich shop, smiling as her friend prattled on about her love life, only to say, "You know, of all the seasons, I think I like fall the best." She invited her friend to look out the window, where leaves were blowing across the parking lot. "I don't know," she continued, absently, "but for some reason days like this make me feel like I'm ten years old again."

Caitlin could see the two of them in the window, looking out.

"You could spend a lifetime," her friend muttered.

———

The news that Alissa would not be coming after all, struck Caitlin broadside, standing, as she was, on the bathroom scale with her clothes off. She had been trying to decide if she had lost any weight in the past week—the scale added three pounds if she leaned slightly to the left, yet dropped two if she rolled onto her heels—when Alissa called.

"A women's shelter?" Caitlin said, "since when do you work at a women's shelter?"

"Mom, I don't work there; I'm a volunteer," Alissa said.

"A volunteer," Caitlin said.

"Anyway, they need me this weekend, and of course I said yes."

Caitlin pictured Alissa putting a blanket around a woman's shoulders, sitting side-by-side on a thin, springless mattress. "But I've already made up your bed," she said.

"Mom, I know you're disappointed, but this is something . . . important."

Important. The word hollowed out a space between them. All at once Caitlin felt horribly naked. She took the phone into the bedroom and slipped into her robe. By the time they said good-bye, she had tucked herself into bed, the robe pulled tightly around her. She did not sleep.

And, that weekend, she attended the Dubois wedding, with the grim determination she sometimes felt when sitting through a bad movie, bent on seeing it to its end. The idea of carrying on pleased her. She would take the day up, she figured, sowing a field of green where there was only clay. In the reception line she hugged the bride too earnestly, as she wiped away tears with the back of her hand.

"I just wish everything *good* for you," she said.

At the reception, she made the rounds, stopping by each table to say hello to friends, and introduce herself to strangers with a warm, overlong handshake. When friends asked about Alissa, she gave a sad click of the tongue, and said, "Alissa couldn't make it." Then, she added an appendage she'd worded in advance.

"She's doing volunteer work," she said, sticking the last two words like push pins.

"Oh," the listener said, repeating it to themselves. "Isn't that wonderful?"

On the dance floor, Caitlin twirled beneath the low gels above, clapping appreciatively whenever the band finished a song. When Tia Godwin's husband, Al, spent the better part of a slow dance apologizing for his clumsiness, Caitlin complimented him on his children, telling him she had always thought them to be remarkable young people. "And I've always thought so," she said.

But when the reception drew to a close—she had been cornered, at this point, by Ellen DuBois, listening to her rhapsodize about the ceremony—she found herself suddenly exhausted. Ellen's husband, Jack, sat with his head to the table, passed out on a stack of napkins. Ellen was recalling how nice the opening prayer was when Caitlin found herself saying," Do you know what my dream would be, Ellen?"

Ellen looked at her, puzzled.

"It would be to live in one house my whole life," she said. "To be born in it, grow up in it, raise children in it, and then leave it for them when I'm gone." She smiled, considering the idea.

Ellen nodded, blankly.

When she stood to retrieve her purse, Jack mumbled, "I liked your dream."

— · —

Outside, the night was gorgeous, starry. Caitlin observed it through the patio window, ready to switch off the lights, when the thought of Alissa stopped her. What was she doing at this moment? It was a silly thing to think about, she knew, sillier, even, because of the stars and the moon, but there it was anyway, showing up uninvited at her patio door. What was she doing? She turned off the lights, but found herself turning them on again, saddened by the sight of the darkened patio. She went upstairs, leaving the lights on.

She entered Alissa's old room, turning on the reading lamp beside the bed. She sat on the bed and pulled out a small, stuffed giraffe she'd hidden under the pillow as a surprise for Alissa. Its dumb black eyes looked out from a soft, lopsided head, its mouth, she now realized, drawn into a frown.

"I agree," she said, and put the toy down. And, in the action of this, a single thought played across her mind, real and inextinguishable.

Alissa would never come home.

She would never sleep in this bed, with its ruffled comforter and extra blanket; she would never read by this lamp. She would go off into the world while Caitlin returned to an empty house, and Alissa to a candlelit apartment, footsteps sounding above. She would send a card at Christmas. She would forget an umbrella in the rain.

Caitlin stood from the bed and smoothed the covers back into place. On her way out the door she turned on a second lamp, then a third.

And, in her bedroom, she did the same, clicking on the tall floor lamp beside her dresser, plugging in a cord to a vanity mirror, its horseshoe of tiny lights winking into life. She left the shower light on, the door pulled back along its runner.

Downstairs, the feeling of turning on five different lights at once—there was a single row of switches along the kitchen wall—pleased her, and Caitlin found herself accompanying the motion with a sound effect.

"Whooosh!" she said, watching the kitchen explode with light.

And, after turning on the final living room light she walked through the house, inspecting her work. She was struck by the way so many empty, neglected spaces were suddenly filled in. She had sometimes noticed this at parties; the way guests stood where she never stood otherwise, sat where she never sat, and gathered themselves into corners only ever visited by a push broom. The refrigerator made somber, gurgling sounds, its door open wide.

Caitlin went outside, dragging the phone from the kitchen. The house sent the adjoining homes into dense shadows, while the sky continued with its wondershow above. She sat at the patio table, cradling the receiver to her shoulder. When Alissa answered, Caitlin felt a tear fall across her knuckles.

"Mom?" Alissa said. "Is that you?"

"Yes."

"Mom, what's wrong? It's past one."

"Tell me about the women," Caitlin said. "I want to hear about the women in the shelter."

"Mom, just tell me what's wrong. Please."

Looking in, Caitlin could see herself in the sliding glass windows, the kitchen lit from inside and out. "Are they sad?"

"Mom," Alissa said.

Caitlin hugged herself against the cold. "Do you get to know them well?"

"Mom, listen, even if I wanted to talk about them I couldn't. It's a rule."

Caitlin bounced her knees beneath the table, trying to calm herself. "Tell me about the beds, then."

"The beds?"

"The beds at the shelter. What are they like?"

And now, in the distance, Caitlin heard something she had not anticipated: the train was passing through town. She listened as it sputtered along, a rumble of boxcars and long, preening whistles.

"They're ordinary beds, Mom," Alissa said, then, hearing silence from the other end, continued, "they're those kind of rickety bunk beds without ladders, you know, like at summer camp." She waited. "Is that what you mean, Mom? Like that?"

Caitlin listened as the train rolled away.

"Yes," she whispered. "Like that."

THE GIRL AT THE STATION

On the day Baker lost his job, he drove by the new gas station on the corner of Elm and Walker Creek. It was a sad-looking station, he thought, despite the red flags webbed between the islands, despite, or perhaps because of, the GRAND OPENING sign slumping from the shop window. These new gas stations lacked a certain charm, Baker thought. But he pulled in anyway.

When Baker inserted his ATM card the pump thanked him, then showed a video of waves lapping a sandy shore. Baker usually enjoyed washing his windows, but here the washer handle was too short: he had to stand on tiptoe to reach across the front windshield. Baker remembered being a kid, watching his father drag the washer above the dashboard, the feeling of that. Sometimes it amazed Baker how much happier he used to feel, but he knew he was too young to think like that. He was only forty-three.

The pump refused to print a receipt; Baker went inside to get one. A girl sat at the register, reading a book. When Baker approached her, she did not look up. "I was wondering if I could get a receipt," he said.

The girl closed the book. "A receipt?" She looked to be about sixteen or seventeen. She had pretty green eyes, but was not otherwise pretty. "Oh. I think it's supposed to give you a receipt."

Funny, the way her eyebrows furrowed, Baker thought. "It told me to ask you for one."

"It?"

"The pump," Baker said.

"The pump told you," the girl said. "Ha." She hid the book beneath the register. Baker wondered if she'd sensed he'd been trying to glimpse its cover. "Let me try something," she said, then turned a key inside the register. "This is only my first day."

"Oh, I'm sorry."

The girl selected a long, copper key from a wide ring. "Don't be. I've been dying to try these keys." She tried several keys.

"Sorry about all this," Baker said.

The girl tried the last key, but no luck. "They say that saying sorry is really an aggressive thing, but I always think it's nice to hear anyway. Where would we be without saying sorry?"

Baker had no answer to that.

"Well, it looks like we'll have to make you a receipt," the girl said. She wrote him a receipt on a carbon ledger, then handed it to him. "There."

"Thanks," Baker said, "for all your trouble."

"I'm supposed to say, 'It's no trouble.'"

When Baker pulled out of the station, he could see the girl reading her book again. She had her feet up on the counter. There had been something in their conversation, Baker thought, but couldn't decide what it was. He drove home, thinking about the word *receipt*. Such a strange word. The silent *p*. The way his brain always wished to confuse it with "recipe." A terrible word, when you stopped and thought about it.

———

Baker lived alone. He'd been married once, divorced, had one child, a daughter, Heather. Heather was fourteen now. She lived with her mother and her mother's new husband, Al, in a town an hour away. She visited Baker twice a month. He and his ex had worked out a deal themselves, without the nastiness of a custody hearing. That was the word his ex-wife, Jean, had used, when they'd sat across the dining room table, dividing up the photographs from the family albums. Nastiness. But how little of their divorce had been nasty. They divided photos with the same ease they'd agreed on visiting schedules, holiday swaps, and summer vacation arrangements. They'd only argued twice, over the framed portraits along the staircase and the Wurlitzer upright Baker had wanted to keep for Heather when she visited. They'd started Heather on piano lessons when she was six; she was pretty good now, although she didn't have the patience to learn new pieces and was shy about playing in front of others. Baker argued that it would be better for them to keep the Wurlitzer at his place so Heather could practice when she visited; Jean said that was ridiculous, since Heather would be spending much more time at her house. The matter was settled by Al, who surprised them all by finding a used baby grand for practically nothing. He'd contacted a local university's music department and inquired. They even delivered it for free. That was just the kind of thing Baker would never think to do. Sometimes, Jean said, it was like he never thought of anything.

"Do you know the only time you're really paying attention?" Jean had asked him, in the months leading up to their separation. "I mean real, honest attention?"

Baker said he didn't know.

"When you're playing with the Macombers' *dog*."

Baker said that wasn't true. But in a way, it was. He loved the Macombers' dog, Teddy. He loved Teddy's attitude. Turn a garden hose on Teddy, he'd wag his tail and eat the spray. Teddy had some things figured out.

"Or reading *Newsweek*," Jean said.

It was hard to tell what people expected of him, Baker wanted to say, but didn't. Sometimes he wanted to ask Heather what she thought about all this, about him, about Jean, about living in two places, but he could never quite bring himself to ask. They had a good little routine going, he thought. He picked Heather up the second and fourth weekends of the month, Heather already waiting in the foyer, gripping a suitcase that always seemed too large for the occasion. Baker would shake hands with Al, then Al would offer Baker a beer and show him the addition he was building off the garage. They'd chat, make jokes, laugh like they were old buddies, which in a way, they'd become, Baker realized. He felt more comfortable around Al than around almost anyone else. How could that be? Sometimes, when Al was explaining a window fixture or drop ceiling, it felt like he was actually saying *But you know how it is with Jean*. "I see what you mean," Baker would say. They'd return to the foyer to find Jean stuffing an extra sweater into Heather's suitcase. When Baker lifted the suitcase, Jean kissed him on the cheek.

It felt strange to have Heather in the house again. Baker wondered if it was strange for her, too. He'd kept her room much the same way it had always been, the scroll-top desk he'd inherited from his grandmother, the stuffed gorilla, the canopy bed they'd once picked out together. Still, the room struck Baker as lonely and empty-looking. The more he added to it—a rocking chair, a corner bookshelf—the emptier it looked. Why?

Once he spent the night there, when Heather was away. The bed was comfortable, the room quiet. The canopy gently suggested that he'd tucked himself into a cloud. Still, he could not sleep. When he finally did, his dreams were troubled. He'd dreamt he'd been enlisted to load luggage onto a passenger plane, moments before it was scheduled to depart. The task was preposterous, but Baker threw himself into it with a rare confidence, sure of himself. He hefted suitcases, steamer trunks, animal cages, golf bags, tuba cases, wheelchairs, baby strollers, heavy duffel bags, all with preternatural speed. The sense of his mission was triumphant; he'd earned the passengers' admiration, although he could not see their faces. Their awe enshrouded him like a gift robe. Baker remembered running down a corridor with a brass lamp in each hand, cords trailing, only to find that the plane had left without him. He stood at the end of the corridor, realizing, for the first time, that he hadn't been asked to load the plane after all, but rather to pilot it.

"Can I take the little TV in here?" Heather asked, on the first night of her visit.

"OK."

"You know I'm not really into stuffed animals anymore, Dad."

"Oh."

"Or dolls." Heather flopped onto the bed. "If this bed was an island," she said. A routine, from her childhood.

"If this bed was an island," Baker said, "the pillows would be rocks."

"If the pillows were rocks, the carpet would be the ocean."

Baker recognized this for what it was: Heather's apology for growing up on him, for leaving him behind. She didn't want to hurt him. That was the thing, Baker realized, no one wanted to hurt him. People looked out for him, like he was someone much younger than he actually was. The girl at the station had written "Official Receipt" at the top of the ledger. She'd underlined this, twice.

Baker took Heather to the movies, but was embarrassed by the movie they'd chosen, a teen comedy whose pranks seemed like something out of a porno flick—or was everything like that now? He'd caught Heather laughing once, at the big moment in the film when the geeky boy seduces the pretty cheerleader, and pretended to laugh along, too, but later regretted this, when they'd left the theater and found it raining outside, a dash to the car, the heater reluctant to warm. They'd driven home in silence. Think of something to say, Baker thought. Something to draw her out. Something just right. He drove through brightly lit neighborhoods whose flagstone walks seemed more neatly trimmed than his own, whose wide driveways seemed the thoroughfares to happier lives, wondering what that possibly might be.

That night Baker awoke. From the living room he could hear Heather playing the piano. The familiar, slightly out of tune Wurlitzer. The music was a joyfully sad piece he felt he'd heard before, then recognized it as Grieg's "Morning Mood." He used to love "Morning Mood." In college he'd play it when no one else was around, the dorm empty, the only sound the needle dropping onto the record. Except this tune was more than "Morning Mood." It was "Morning Mood"'s twin. The melody was the same, but better somehow, improved. It led the listener through unseen rooms, warmer, more substantial than the ones Grieg had arranged. Every note seemed to ask *Do you see?* and answer *Yes, it is* all at the same time.

In college, Baker had kept his record player beside his bed. Whenever he had a girl in his room, he played a record. Most of the time he'd play something new, rock or jazz, but every once in a while, if he felt a bit more comfortable around the girl, he'd play something classical. That was how things had started with Jean. They'd met in a history class, Greek Civilization, Professor Bauer, whose frail, faltering voice seemed somehow caught up in the slow movement of Mahler's Fifth, or the opening measures of Wagner's Lohengrin. It was for Jean that Baker had first played Grieg's Peer Gynt. It was for her he'd dropped the needle to "Morning Mood." She sat on his bed after they'd made love, listening. "What is it?" she asked. Baker told her. Later, she surprised him by straddling him again. They made a joke about it, later. "Morning Mood," they'd say, and laugh. A secret phrase. Could it be that she'd told Heather? Impossible, Baker thought.

The next morning Baker asked, "Were you playing the piano last night?"

"Last night?" Heather shook her head. "No."

"Really?"

Heather gave him a look. "Duh, Dad, I think I'd remember." She shook Cheerios into a bowl.

"Because I'm not angry about it. Not at all," Baker said. "I thought it sounded wonderful."

Heather poured milk onto her cereal.

"You're getting better and better," Baker said.

Heather read the back of the Cheerios box. A maze Baker had already filled in. "Whatever," she said. She turned the box around, idly. "I mean thanks, I guess."

———

A week after he lost his job, Baker had an appointment with a temp agency. He showed up in a suit he hadn't worn in nine years and shoes he'd Windexed over the kitchen sink.

"Let's see," his agent said, glancing over his resume. "You've listed your Microsoft proficiency as 'intermediate.' Tell me, can you do a mail merge?"

"A mail merge?"

"Yes, you've heard of those?" The agent had a stray hair caught in her glasses. Baker wondered if he should say something.

"Sure. I mean yes I have, but no, I haven't done one." Baker felt his face grow warm. "But I'm sure I could, with the book."

"The book? The instruction manual?"

"Yes."

"OK," the agent said, then crossed something out. "I'm going to put down 'beginner.'"

Baker spent the next hour in the presence of a wizard. The wizard, dressed in a flowing purple robe, led Baker through a typing test, a reading test, a math test, a logic skills test, and a computer aptitude exam. His starry wand, which sometimes made an approving ding like a tricycle's bell, accompanied Baker out of the office and into the rest of his day. Ding-ding! The agent had a nice voice, Baker thought. Comforting, but stern. Lately it seemed to Baker that he was a little bit in love with nearly every woman he met, but maybe he'd always been that way and hadn't taken the time to notice. That was a consolation about losing your job and driving around the business loop trying to run low on gas—you really noticed things.

Baker pulled into the gas station. The girl stood outside the shop door, smoking a cigarette.

"Isn't that dangerous?" Baker said.

"A little," she said. She mashed the cigarette out with her sneaker. After a while she asked, "Were you driving around here earlier?"

"I've been driving around all morning trying to run out of gas."

"Ha," the girl said.

They talked. The girl was in community college, not high school, as Baker had thought. Business major, but didn't like it all that much. Sort of boring. She'd wanted to be a botanist, but oh well. Maybe after retirement. Laughter.

"Sounds exotic," Baker said.

"I used to work in a flower shop," the girl said.

They talked about jobs without Baker mentioning his. He liked it that she didn't ask, either. He liked that about a person, when they didn't ask you what you did for a living. That had always felt to him like they were really asking, So, who are you? when, as long as he could remember, none of his jobs felt like him. Not even close. Even the wizard wanted to know. The wizard! That had been a way to spend his morning! Now he was with the girl at the station, talking about geraniums, the new shopping mall, Heather. It was amazing how much better everything was when you didn't have to show up at eight in the morning with a smile screwed onto your face. Baker didn't even have to say good morning to anyone he didn't want to anymore. Old peelings seemed to fall from him like a stripped door.

The girl liked hearing about Heather. She laughed when Baker told her about Heather's sixth-grade piano recital, when she'd stopped in the middle of a Bach partita to remove the satiny pink ribbon her teacher had tied into her hair. He told her about Heather without quite mentioning that he was divorced, that he spent far less time with her than he let on, that he and Heather spent what little time they had together going to movies, driving home in silence. The Heather he described was strong-willed, but kind; talented, but shy to acknowledge it. The Heather he described was someone perhaps not too unlike her father, who was only too glad to praise the way she befriended the most unpopular kids at school, poets and dreamers like herself, who was rarely embarrassed to be seen with her parents, tossing a bag of chips into their shopping cart. He did not mention the loneliness he'd felt watching Heather eat her cereal. His secret worry that she resented visiting him. His fear that she did not exactly love him anymore. He did not mention "Morning Mood," nor Heather's lie about it.

"I'd like to meet her sometime," the girl at the station said.

That night Baker stayed up until two in the morning listening to old records and drinking a bottle of wine. He'd intended to donate the records to the local library, but the library had apologetically refused them. No demand for records anymore. Baker had dragged the boxes back into the garage, and now made a little adventure out of walking to the garage, selecting one record at a time, then returning inside with the chill of garage floor still lingering between his toes. Baker drank the last of the wine straight from the bottle, then drank another. On his last trip to the garage, he saw a mouse dart behind the lawnmower.

———

Baker started his first temp job. "We'll set you up with a phone and a directory," his supervisor said. She handed Baker a green folder. "These will help you." Inside, a directory of business people, contact numbers, short bios, photographs. Baker scanned a few of these, men in ties, women with unfashionable hair. "Feel free to call whomever you like," the woman continued. "But try to contact at least ten potential customers an hour." She led Baker to a cubicle. "You can use Richard's phone today." The cubicle was festooned with comic strips. Some of them looked thirty years old. Yellow. "Let us know if you have any questions."

Richard's phone was tricky, but Baker eventually got the hang of it. His assignment was to call executives and invite them to a trade show. Simple. No sales, the agency had promised. Only "courtesy calls." Baker couldn't argue; he needed the money.

"I hear you, I hear you," his first caller said, "but listen, I don't go to that kind of crap anymore. You know?"

"Sure," Baker said. "I understand."

"All those name tags, all that boozing and schmoozing. That's a young man's game, right?"

"Right," Baker said.

"But good luck to you. You're bound to get some takers."

"Thanks."

Baker flipped through the directory, looking for receptive faces. Smiling faces, he discovered, were twice as likely to say yes. If someone had an especially nice smile—Barbara Knox, page 14, for example—he'd leave a message on their machine. By noon he'd gotten a dozen people to agree to come to the trade show. "Great. I'll look forward to seeing you there," he found himself saying, even though he knew this was ridiculous. "We're expecting a terrific turnout." His voice sounded strange to him, both artificial and earnest. He liked the possibility of people asking about him at the trade show. It's good to be here, they'd say. Now—where's Baker?

Baker was eating his lunch in Richard's cubicle when the telephone rang. "Hello?" Baker said, then realized he should have said, "Good afternoon," as he'd been instructed. That didn't seem natural to Baker.

There was a pause on the other end. The sound of a TV in the background.

"Hello?" Baker said.

"Daddy?" A child's voice.

"Hi there," Baker said. "Who's this?"

"*Daddy*," the child said, with such recognition that Baker was taken off guard. It was a little girl's voice.

"Hi," he said.

"Daddy, whazza home?"

Baker didn't say anything. He felt his throat tighten.

"Whazza home?"

Baker looked around to make sure no one else was listening. "Sweetheart, listen. Can you hang up the phone for Daddy?'

"Whazza home?"

"Daddy's going to hang up now. But he'll be home soon, OK. Say bye-bye? Bye-bye?"

"Bye-bye."

"Bye-bye." He felt guilty for hanging up without saying he loved her. Wasn't that funny? After work, Baker paid a surprise visit to Heather. He pulled into the driveway, thinking of ways to tell her about his silly new job, the directory, the little girl calling for her daddy. Heather might like the story about the girl. Together, they might laugh about it.

"Hey stranger," Al said, opening the front door. He told Baker that Heather and Jean had gone to the mall. Would Baker like a beer? They drank two apiece, sitting in the screened-in porch, which Al had recently finished and fitted out with a gas grill. The beer reminded Baker of the two bottles of wine he'd drunk the night of the records. What a dumb thing to do. He thought about telling Al about it, but didn't. More and more Baker felt like he had things to say, but no idea how to say them.

"They'll be gone a while, I'm afraid," Al said.

"Oh," Baker said. He wondered if this was a hint for him to leave. He had a hard time picking up hints sometimes.

"Heather's looking for a dress."

"Oh." Baker told Al he'd better be getting along anyway, then got back on the road. Watching the house disappear in the rearview mirror, Baker wondered if Heather sometimes thought of Al as her father. He bet she did, in a way. In a way, he couldn't blame her. Then he wondered if Jean thought Al was better in bed, but he didn't like thinking about that, so he didn't. Heather would have liked the story about the little girl. But it would have made her sad, too. That was the thing about Heather, Baker thought, she could always see the sad in things. That's what he'd heard in "Morning Mood," but couldn't quite place, the sadness. It really was a sad tune, when you listened.

It was late by the time Baker got home. In bed, he read a magazine without any comprehension of what he was reading, then turned out the light. But it didn't seem dark enough to sleep. A mean trick. Baker turned on his side and buried his face beneath a pillow. He'd never realized how odorous sheets got when you hadn't washed them in a while. Come to think of it, he hadn't washed much of anything in a while. He'd been drinking ice water from old jelly jars. Eating cereal from plastic spoons. A ripped grocery bag held weeks of unread mail.

Whazza home?

A few weeks after Baker started his temp job, Heather graduated from eighth grade. The school held a ceremony in the gymnasium, where Baker stood with the other parents and snapped a photograph when Heather received her diploma. Later he drove her to a restaurant for a celebratory meal. Heather was dressed up in a pretty green dress; her mother had allowed her to wear makeup, earrings, a fake string of pearls. Heather spent the drive flipping the dashboard vents, changing the radio stations every other minute. Baker wondered if her mother had to talk her into going to dinner with him. The idea depressed him.

"They really had the gym all decked out, didn't they?" he said.

Heather shrugged. "I can't believe you used a disposable camera," she said. She twirled the camera from its string.

"My Minolta is on the fritz," Baker apologized.

Heather snapped a picture of herself. "At least the flash works," she said.

Baker had forgotten to make a dinner reservation. The first restaurant they tried told them to expect an hour wait, the second an hour and a half, the third was so busy that Heather tugged on Baker' sleeve and said, "Let's just go," before Baker could ask the hostess. "Sorry," Baker said, when they pulled out of the parking lot. "I should have made a reservation."

"Like, ten schools are having their graduation tonight," Heather said. "Every place will be packed."

"We'll find a place," Baker said, but Heather didn't say anything.

They drove the business loop, where Baker had so often gone, hoping to see the girl at the station. The station was busy tonight, cars at every island, teenagers milling about the parking lot. Everything was busy tonight. Every car at every stoplight was driven by a teenage boy with his arm slung loosely out the window, it seemed to Baker. At an intersection, a passenger in the car next to him signaled Baker to roll his window down. "Um, excuse me," he said. He wore a baseball cap and a necklace made of tiny shells. His eyes were pink. "But my friend and I were kinda wondering: do you need sex?" The boy behind the wheel pitched forward, laughing. Baker rolled his window up and drove through the intersection.

"Great night," Heather said.

"Those jerks," Baker said.

"Yeah."

The world was getting more crude, it was true. How Baker wished to protect Heather. How hopeless it all sometimes seemed, being a father, wishing things. He wanted to say he was sorry for everything, but Heather turned the radio up, then stared out the passenger window at the bright nothing passing by. Why hadn't he made dinner reservations?

"We can just go to Denny's," Heather said.

"We can't go to Denny's on your graduation night. Not Denny's."

Heather shrugged. "I'm starving."

"We'll try the Winston Grill."

But the Winston Grill was now a Walgreen's. When had the Winston Grill gone under? "I can't believe it," Baker said.

"They've been gone since forever," Heather said. She gave way to an exasperated sigh, a leftover habit from her childhood, recalling, to Baker's mind, Sunday afternoons at the Wurlitzer, rain sheeting against the living room windows, Monday's exercise still unlearned.

"I'm sorry, honey," Baker said.

"It's not your fault," Heather said.

"But it is," Baker said. "It's completely my fault"

Heather put her hands to her head. "God!" she said. "Why does everyone think everything is their fault? You and mom are both the same. You feel guilty for everything."

Baker made no argument. He did feel guilty for everything.

"I'm sorry," he said.

"That's another thing: stop saying sorry," Heather said. "Look, it's just a dumb graduation ceremony with dumb speeches and a dumb dress and everyone running around trying to make it 'special.' Oh, it's so 'special.' Well, no, it's not. OK? It's no big deal. It's just a night like any other night and I'm hungry and I'd just as soon go home." She wiped a tear from her eye. "Plus this dress is killing me."

They drove for a while without speaking. Baker thought about pulling into Denny's, but decided against it. Even Denny's looked overcrowded. "Would you like to come home with me?" Baker asked. "I have a frozen pizza in the fridge. It has pepperoni on it, but I could scrape those off. They practically fall off anyway."

"Dad," Heather said. "Look, it's OK. We can take a rain check or whatever."

"A rain check?"

"Yeah, we'll do something next time. It's not a big deal."

Baker considered this. "If we do, it won't be your graduation night anymore. You do realize that, don't you?"

"Oh, tragedy," Heather said.

"You know, you shouldn't say it isn't a big deal because it is. It's a huge deal."

"Fine," Heather said. "It's a huge deal."

"I mean it," Baker said. He looked over at Heather, but she was examining her string of pearls. She had her chin down, eyebrows raised, a gesture Baker recognized as one of Jean's. Well, he had failed Jean, and now he would fail Heather, too. There was no way around it. Heather would be kind to him, excusing his shortcomings, forgiving him over and over, just as Jean had done, just as everyone had done, it seemed. On the day he was fired his supervisor took him aside, pacing the office where Baker sometimes loitered, where they had watched ball games on the tiny television they'd once purchased together, dragging a hand through his thinning hair.

"Goddamn it all," he'd said. "Dan wants you out of here. I'm not supposed to say anything, but there it is."

Baker told him he understood, not to worry, he sort of knew it was coming anyway.

"If there was anything I could do, I'd do it. But."

"Did he say why?"

"Yeah. He said he thinks we've all been letting you 'slide along' for too long."

Baker spent the rest of that morning in the office stairwell, trying to imagine what it would be like to be fired. When he couldn't imagine anything, he returned to his desk to find Dan looking for him. "Baker," Dan said.

The station was busy, bright. Baker didn't see the girl behind the register, but pulled into the far island and told Heather he'd be right back. Inside, Baker saw two women working the register, neither of them the girl. "Excuse me," he said, "but is the other girl working tonight?"

"Who?"

Baker described her. This was harder to do than he thought. You had to talk about hair, eyes. You couldn't say the girl who makes me feel strangely at ease. The way I wish I could be around everyone, but never seem to manage.

"He means Sarah," the other woman said. *Sarah*.

"Crazy Sarah?" the first woman said. "She said she's gonna stop by and pick up her paycheck. You want me to tell her you stopped by?"

"No, that's OK," Baker said. He felt suddenly ridiculous. "I'll stop by some other time." He bought nine dollars worth of soda, candy, and salty snacks, then handed these to Heather. "To tide you over," he explained.

"What are we doing here?" Heather asked.

"There's someone I'd like you to meet."

"Here?"

"Here."

Together they watched people going in and out of the shop. They split a Snickers bar and a king-sized bag of peanut M&M's. It was amazing how good peanut M&M's were, Baker thought. They polished those off, then started in on the Nutter Butters and Twizzlers. Twizzlers were more of Heather's thing, but Baker didn't mind. They made fun of teenage boys trying to buy beer, then walking out with Gatorade and Mountain Dew.

"Will I know him when I see him?" Heather asked.

"Her," Baker said. "Sarah."

"Oh, Christ, is she your new girlfriend or something? Because I really don't think I'm ready for something like that."

"She's not my girlfriend," Baker said. He told her about the girl.

Heather took a swallow of Yoo-hoo. "Thank God." She wiped her mouth with a paper napkin. "You know, I bet I'll recognize her," she said. "Sarah. I can see her now."

And she did. She pointed her out to Baker, who hadn't noticed her at all. She was dressed differently, in jeans and a gray T-shirt, her hair pulled back into a baseball cap. "That's her, right?" Heather said.

Baker nodded.

"Anyone could tell," Heather said.

They watched as Sarah went inside the shop, talked with the other women. She was describing something the other women thought funny. She filled a soda from the fountain and drank it without a lid.

"Have you been hanging out with her or something?" Heather asked.

"No," Baker said, "it's not like that."

"She's kind of pretty," Heather said.

Baker felt he should try to explain. "She reads," he said, but that didn't sound right.

"I bet she'll see us," Heather said. She took a long drink, laughed. "She'll think we're up to something."

A moment later Sarah pushed through the shop door. She tossed her soda into a trash can, held the door for a mother holding a baby. Baker watched, wondering if she really would spot them after all. Insects treaded air noiselessly above the windshield, their wings brilliant beneath the station lights. Maybe we're invisible, Baker thought. He wasn't sure if the idea pleased or disappointed him. He sensed Heather's breathing as an extension of his own, and was surprised when Heather rolled her window down and said, "Sarah, over here," to which Sarah turned her gaze on them without really seeing them, it seemed, until Heather called out, "It's us," and Baker saw Sarah raise her hand and knew she understood.

LEAVING THE MOVIES

The summer I was sixteen I worked at a movie theater. The theater was old, poorly patronized, and rumored to be tied to the mob, although I could never imagine my boss, Mr. Jolls, to be connected to that sort of thing. Mr. Jolls was nearly sixty, soft-spoken, and had a habit of wearing bath slippers around the office, which he'd decorated with pictures of birds. Sometimes I'd hang out in his office when there was nothing to do and he'd tell me about birds he and his wife had spotted together. They'd kept a list of these. When he spoke, Mr. Jolls sometimes closed his eyes like a tipped doll, which took some getting used to. But I liked him. At night, he let us climb the marquee and drink sodas we'd filled from the concession stand. From the marquee I could see my high school, whose stadium lights shone brightly upon the marching band I'd neglected to join. Sometimes I could hear them, a sudden brass fanfare or drum cadence rising, then subsiding, like a passing train.

The movie theater was my first job. I'd applied because some friends of mine were working there already, but one of them left before I started and the other, Randy, spent most of his time trying to seduce Janet, a beautiful college girl who worked the ticket office. Randy's sudden change in loyalties, the way he sometimes used me as the butt of a joke, was my first lesson in adult compromise, although I didn't know it at the time. I took to acting like I didn't care. I'd wipe the concession stand counter with a damp rag, imagining scenes where I'd confront Randy with his betrayal, reducing him to a cowering, crying heap on the floor. Other times I'd tug trash bags from their sticky barrels, then heave them into a rusty dumpster, all the while imagining Randy begging me for my attention. "You don't understand," he'd say. "I love her."

"Love," I'd say, then heave another bag. "That's a good one." I'd climb into the dumpster, as we had been instructed to do, and stomp the bags down, indifferent to Randy's protestations. "That's a real good one."

My idea of myself was wrapped up in the movies, but I wouldn't admit that, either. I made a habit of bringing a book with me whenever I worked as an usher. *Fahrenheit 451*, *Catcher in the Rye*, *A Separate Peace* were particular favorites. *A Separate Peace* was slender enough to fit inside the pocket of my pleated twill pants, black, and smelling of popcorn grease no matter how many times my mother laundered them. I kept *A Separate Peace* in the same pocket where I also kept my key ring, since the key ring would help raise the book above the lip of the pocket. I always hoped some girl would notice and ask me out for coffee, a hope which was also cribbed from the movies, as was my idea of being discovered by a talent scout, impressed by me reading *A Night to Remember* by flashlight during a ten o'clock screening of *The Goonies*. I had some idea

of myself as a screenwriter. Or a philosopher-poet. For my sixteenth birthday, I'd asked for the complete recordings of Rob-
ert Lowell. My parents got me a gift certificate to Sam Goody.

Part of my job was to prevent people from putting their
feet on the seats. I hated this part of the job. I'd never been
good at asserting myself. I was a mumbler, a blusher, a keeper
of journals. But the flashlight helped, as did the anonymity the
movie screen temporarily granted: the bright light made a sil-
houette of me, me with my flashlight flickering across the tops
of their Keds, Nikes, Docksiders.

"Feet, please," I'd say. Usually the person wouldn't hear
me until I'd repeated myself again.

"What did he say?"

"Feet, please."

One woman angrily told me, "We're not putting our feet
down until you get rid of the *roaches* in here!"

"Amen," her boyfriend said. He was drinking from a bag.
We found bottle bags all the time. Bacardi, usually.

"Or get yourself some bleach," the woman said. "Floor's
like flypaper down there."

"You're telling some truths," the husband said.

"I know I am," the woman said.

I did what I always did when confronted: acquiesced. "I'll
see what I can do about that," I said, then walked to the back
of the theater, where the feeling of pushing through the two
swinging doors into the little corridor that separated the theater from the lobby was like stepping through a sprinkler on
a hot summer day. The corridor was lit by a trio of dim lights;
it was under these that I followed Guy Montag into hiding,
Holden to Phoebe's bedroom, and Phineas across a jounced
limb. I'd read until I heard the closing credits, then open the
double doors, where people staggered out with their fists
clenching jackets, Sno-Caps. I always liked waiting for this
moment, since I could trick myself into thinking that I was
somehow releasing these people from the theater, that their
averted glances and tossed wrappers were a silent thank you.

We thought we'd never escape, their discarded sodas seemed to say. How can we ever repay you?

It was usually during one of these waits that Alan appeared. Alan was in his forties, married with two children, although he was shy to talk about them. Short, wire hanger thin, with thick eyebrows that suggested constant surprise, Alan made a ritual of vacuuming the theater with a manual sweeper. The sweeper was orange and white, with two compartments that could be opened like a steamed crab, revealing a tangle of lint, dust, and crushed popcorn. Alan's Sweeper, we called it. The sweeper made a low, clicking noise whenever he raced across the lobby to vacuum a cluster of dropped popcorn or rid the floor of a torn ticket stub.

"You been reading this whole time?"

"Not the whole time."

Alan dropped his voice. "You better not let the Big Shots catch you with that," he said. "They'll give you the slip."

"I've got my eye out."

"That's what they all think," Alan said, "then the next thing—" he made a slashing motion across his throat. "The end."

The Big Shots were one of Alan's main preoccupations. Every three weeks or so, the theater owner, Big Steven, would stop by, his young-looking wife, Madeleine, in tow. They'd chat with Mr. Jolls for a while, Big Steven poking his finger into Mr. Jolls's chest, saying, "Harry, goddamned if you don't get fatter every time I see you," while Mr. Jolls put his hands up as if to say, Well, what can you do? "You're soft, Harry," Big Steven would say, "But that's what I like about you, right?" There was a false note in Mr. Jolls's agreement, as there was in his absurd smile, which hung a sudden web of wrinkled skin from the corners of his eyes. "Did you hear what I said to this guy, honey? I said that's what I like about him."

"We heard you," Madeleine said. "We all heard you, you big blowhard."

"That's the respect I get," Big Steven said. "See?" he said, turning to me, "How many times I gotta tell you: don't get married."

It was usually in the middle of one of these awkward visits that Alan would appear, pushing his sweeper. He made a show of getting the places underneath the poster board cut-outs no one ever thought to move. It was funny watching him lift Arnold Schwarzenegger like he weighed nothing at all.

"Alan, my God," Big Steven would say, "if only I had twenty of you." And there would follow a conversation in which Madeleine brightened, asking Alan about his wife, his kids, how his back was holding up. The three of them talked for a while, their conversation adopting the feeling of a private business meeting where Alan was somehow treated as the manager, while Mr. Jolls looked on. It was strange, watching Alan's pleasure in their conversation, his sudden confidence, especially since he wore a wrinkled usher's jacket from which his name-tag hung like a smacked mailbox, while Big Steven wore a three-button suit and Madeleine leaned against the concession stand in high-heeled shoes that strained against their leather straps. Alan's teeth were lousy, too, and I felt embarrassed for him whenever he turned an enormous, thankful smile upon Madeleine, who always helped herself to the popcorn, offering it to us all like we hadn't been feasting on it all night. I liked Madeleine, though. She was pretty. Red hair, green eyes, and pale skin that nurtured dozens of freckles across her arms. I sometimes fantasized about sleeping with her. One of my biggest fears was that someone would notice, and I would break into an uncontrollable blush.

Big Steven's visit would end with him taking us on a tour of the theater. He'd walk with his hands folded over his chest, explaining, at a nearly breathless pace, our negligence in several key areas. We'd let a soap dispenser run dry, forgotten to stack the popcorn topping boxes label out to assist us during inventory, ignored the moth graveyards growing inside the marquee globes, left tape marks across the lobby window, kept too many cleansers near the candy stock, mispositioned the

Las Vegas Sweepstakes Giveaway display, referred to golden topping as "butter," as in "Would you like butter on that?," left the dumpster unlocked, left a palette jack on the loading dock, left a bottle of roach spray on the fire steps in full customer view, worn black jeans instead of black khakis, failed to promote the gift certificates between showings, and hadn't alerted mall security to the kids loitering in the parking lot as we had been advised to do. "Plus it's fucking freezing in here," he said. "Can't even feel my goddamned toes."

It was cold. It was always cold. The air conditioner sometimes ran for days on end without stopping.

"The air conditioner is broken," Alan said.

"It never stops," I explained.

For a while, we'd been able to staunch the flow by jamming a screwdriver into the thermostat; we kept a quartz heater hidden behind Mr. Jolls's desk.

"Well, it's going to start working," Big Steven said. He made us follow him to the utility room, where the thermostat still wore a sign Randy had fashioned out of a *Lethal Weapon* poster and pasted Red Hots. C A N ' T S T O P D A F R E E Z E ! ! the Red Hots read, haloing around Danny Glover's head. Janet had helped Randy make it look symmetrical.

"What the hell is this?" Big Steven said. He tore the sign off. "Is this what you people do when you're on the clock? Make silly crap?"

I looked down, as did everyone else. A shared thought stretched between us like an enormous, invisible web: *please don't let him find the Jujube robot in the mop room.*

"Because that's not what you're paid to do, is it?"

We agreed that it wasn't.

But it was hard to say what was. My shift started at one. I'd punch in, pin my nametag to my vest, fill a forty-two-ounce cup with half Dr. Pepper, half Cherry Coke, then hang out in Mr. Jolls's office until Alan materialized in the office door, saying, "We need someone on tickets," which was my cue to tuck my shirt in, swallow one last gulpful of Cherry Pepper, and unlock the lobby doors, where, already, kids were waiting, their parents pulling away in station wagons. The lobby doors were tinted; I could see the kids before they saw me. They sat on the curb with their T-shirts stretched across their knees, tube socks bunched down to ankles, punching each other on the shoulder (boys) or whispering, hands held to each other's ears (girls). There was always a moment when I first turned the key in the lock that the kids would look at me, but still not be able to see me. They'd be looking right at me and not even know it. I always liked this moment, because their expressions revealed something I did not expect: disappointment. Regret. Sorrow. Like I was the principal opening the doors to summer school! But then I'd swing the doors open and the kids would pass me by, laughing, joking, like there was no place they'd rather be. They'd scramble to the ticket office where Janet reprimanded them if they tried to pay with pennies. They'd drop popcorn all the way into the theater, Alan trailing behind like a sailboat's rudder.

It was my job to tear tickets. "Thank you," I'd say, if I was tearing an adult's ticket, or "Enjoy the show," if they were senior citizens. But for the kids I didn't say anything. Many of them were barely younger than me. Their hands were always sweaty. They rarely looked at me. Usually the boys would be staring back at Janet, making comments about her. Or they'd be bragging about how many times they'd already seen the movie they were about to see. You could never tell which kind of boy was going to be which, a Janet Boy or a Bragger Boy. One time this skinny kid with horrible acne dropped to one knee and proposed to Janet while his friends looked on, laughing so hard they began to cry. I grabbed the kid by his sleeve just as Janet leaned into the microphone and said, "Tell him I said yes." I took the kid to the bench and gave him a speech about not pulling crap like that. How he could be banned from the theater forever. How we would call his parents and let them know. How we'd call his friends' parents, too. Don't think we wouldn't call his friends' parents, too. But the kid only studied his shoes, dragging the toe of his sneaker across the floor. "But she said yes," he said.

My next job was to usher the rows. After that, wait around until the movie ended so we could clean the theater for the next show. Cleaning was little more than a few pulls on a push broom and a hasty sweep with a wet mop, but I got into it anyway. There's a certain pleasure in mopping a floor, especially one as dirty as the theater was. I'd fill the bucket with a mixture of hot water and Lime-Away!, a cheap industrial detergent the color of anti-freeze, then drag it to the end of each row, racing against a song in my head. I liked doing that. I liked pretending my task was tremendously important. I imagined the floor being afraid of me, me and my mop, whose head sprouted thick braids like a sheepdog, and whose handle made a clicking noise whenever I maneuvered it into a tricky spot. I liked the way the water evaporated almost immediately after I'd left the row, leaving whorls of Lime-Away! like a Van Gogh sky.

But how long the wait was until cleaning time! My job was nothing more than waiting around for the next cleaning time, an idea that suddenly seemed to me the larger truth about the world: there was too much time in it. Our job: kill it. The signs of our slayings were everywhere. We'd hidden a pipe of linked drinking straws, twenty feet long, in the ceiling tiles above the break room. For a while, we'd been diligent about adding to the pipe, Randy standing on a wobbly chair while Janet fed him handful after handful of red and white straws, but after a while we lost interest. We'd fashioned a bobsled out of trash can wheels and postal sorting bins, which we'd been in the habit of racing down the center aisle when Mr. Jolls wasn't around, but even that became tiresome, especially after one of the wheels refused to spin. We'd made a collage on the back of Mr. Jolls's office door. The collage was composed of mismatched eyes, noses, mouths, heads, ears from various movie posters. Looking into it, on a night when Mr. Jolls was gone and everyone else was watching Randy throw the Jujube robot off the roof, I had that sudden, terrible, creepy feeling I sometimes had as a kid when I'd press my nose to the bathroom mirror and open my eyes wide, staring myself down. Like I was someone I didn't know. Someone who wished myself harm, even. I slammed the office door and raced to the rooftop, where Randy had just released the Jujube robot, its Jujube head separating from its Jujube body in midair. This disappointed Randy, as did the failure of the parking lot to send the robot into a thousand pieces. We would have thrown him again if Alan hadn't materialized from the fire exit and scooped him into a trash can.

I kept my bicycle on the projection room stairs. When my shift was over, I'd walk it across the lobby, where the exit door was always heavier than I expected. I'd nudge its heavy bar with my hips, then mount the bicycle all in one motion. The door would slam behind me, and suddenly I'd be pedaling across the parking lot. It was summer; the nights were warm. The air informed me that I'd been freezing all evening without even knowing it. I'd hear cars passing on the highway, see trucks pulling into the Acme supermarket lot, and feel I was getting away with something. Escaping. The bike gears clicked whenever I let the bike coast free. I'd feel the vibration in my legs.

I was old enough to drive, but didn't have a car. My father would sometimes loan me his Impala, but I always felt nervous driving it, since the Impala was the car that had picked me up from so many swim practices, friends' homes, rainy bus stops, my head covered with a held notebook. Driving it would be like reading the business section while listening to MacNeil/ Lehrer. So I took my bike. We lived a mile and a half from the theater, our neighborhood arranged along a long, sloping hill that ascended to the shopping center. The ride up the hill was laborious, hot, a chore. I tried to stay on the shady side of the street, but on the hottest days of July it hardly mattered. Sweat beaded upon my back, a new thing for me, as were the tiny black hairs around my navel, dewed with moisture. My attentions narrowed to the tire treading the sidewalk before me. I imagined onlookers cheering me on. They applauded when I rode beneath the spray of a lawn sprinkler, but grew concerned when I nearly stopped pedaling at the base of Worley Avenue, the steepest slope of the hill. Worley. My pedaling took on its name, WOR-LEY, WOR-LEY, as did the breath heaving in my chest. I'd reach the stop sign at the top of the hill and mop my face with the hem of my shirt. My hands exuded the smell of foam rubber.

But leaving the theater was different. Nighttime lent me a feeling of invisibility, as did my speed, me rocketing down the neighborhood streets without ever needing to pedal. The neighborhood, which had earlier seemed a trick ramp, raised higher and higher as I neared its edge, now offered itself up like an unwrapped gift. Houses, earlier ignored, now cast long bars of light across my path, their porches, I now saw, stacked with firewood. Lawns freckled with stray toys, trampolines, garden hoses, birdbaths, hockey sticks, kiddie pools reflecting streetlights back to themselves like compact mirrors. I stood on the pedals and felt the wind in my hair. When I reached the top of Worley, I'd take the street as fast as I could, riding down the center where the pavement was smooth, free of cracks. Sometimes, if there were no cars around, I'd close my eyes. It was always surprising to see where I was when I opened them again, since I pictured myself to be perilously close to the bottom of the avenue when really I hadn't gone very far at all. I'd make little bargains with myself, like *If I make it to the end of this lawn with my eyes closed, that means I'll be famous.* But I always chose the easiest challenges, winning every time. I'd win fame, money, longevity a thousand times over in the time it took to turn the corner onto Bradley Street and pedal past the blue fire hydrant whose bolts had been painted to look like eyes and a nose.

I liked to imagine myself as someone welcome in every house, even though I didn't know any of the neighbors along my route. I liked to picture myself stopping by anyway, saying hello. Just on my way home, I'd say to whomever cared to ask. Beautiful night. These fantasies didn't seem farfetched to me, since I already felt myself to be someone who would one day own a house like these, too. A modest home with a two-car garage and a landscaped drive. Maybe a pool; maybe not. I still hadn't decided. Nothing pretentious, though, like the purple and cream Victorian at the corner of Ridge Run, with all those turrets angling toward the sky like windowed rockets. No. My house would be simple, honest. That's what the neighbors understood about me. I kept it simple. I sped by house after house, feeling their approval. This feeling, so hidden through-out the day, so absent during my shift at the theater, seemed to me the feeling all my other actions tended toward, like a plant angling toward the sun. I rounded the corner to my street, and felt I was somehow deeply loved.

When I got home, I often found my mother asleep on the sofa. Her breathing saddened me, as did the TV applauding itself for no one. I'd leave my shoes on the garage steps, where my socks from the day before lay curled into balls. Upstairs, bed. My fan turning its breath across my feet.

—

The third weekend in July, Big Steven reassigned Mr. Jolls to a different theater. For failure to increase ticket sales. As a step toward retirement. For failing to unlock the fire doors during a matinee check—or so Alan said. We never got the full story. What we did get was Anton, our new boss. He appeared on a Monday morning, standing atop the concession stand, above which a rectilinear sign hung from two short chains. Anton had his shirtsleeves rolled to his elbows, his left hand steadying the sign, while his right roved inside: the sign had a removable back panel, it seemed. "Good morning," he said, spotting me. He had a faint European accent.

"Hi."

"I think this goes, eh—" he strained to see inside the sign, "I think this goes off and on?" He wore expensive-looking dress shoes, but had neglected socks. He looked barely thirty. "There!" He stood back to admire the sign, whose border now blinked in a hypnotic, alternating pattern. It was like discovering that your cat, if petted a certain way, would voluntarily tap dance.

"We had no idea," I said.

"It's a big excitement, eh?" Anton said. A moment later he fixed the hot dog rotisserie so that its carousel no longer squeaked.

By noon we'd learned his whole story. He was from Holland originally, but had grown up in Germany before moving to the United States. He'd gone to college, but had dropped out after his twins were born. He planned to return someday and finish his degree in chemical engineering. He told us this while sitting apologetically behind Mr. Jolls's desk, where a snowy egret paperweight still stood. "Do we like these?" he said, gesturing toward the paperweight.

"Mr. Jolls liked birds," Janet said.

Anton considered this. Then he said, "The birds stay!" as if we'd been debating this all along.

Anton's philosophy, as we soon learned, was that each of us should be able to do every job in the theater. So Anton took me to the projection room and had Randy explain how to load the reels, sound loop facing out, so that the transition between each was seamless. I learned how to dim the preview lights at just the right moment, how to use the public address system, how to prevent the films from moisture damage, how to splice a twisted frame—as did Janet, Alan, and the concession stand workers. It was strange, hanging out with Randy again. All summer we'd barely spoken, Randy dropping his voice two octaves lower than normal, trying to sound cool and mysterious in case Janet was nearby. I dropped my voice, too, in some show of solidarity, and, in this way, we mumbled our friendship back together, mostly over my mistakes, like the time I accidentally switched the preview volume to ten, and sent parents running to the lobby, their hands shielding their children's ears. I worked the ticket office with Janet. I vacuumed the lobby floors with Alan's Sweeper. I scooped popcorn, rotated the candy stock, and learned how to fill three sodas at once so that their filling coincided with the nacho tray bubbling inside the microwave. I got good at counting back change. *That's one and two and three forty-five.* The pleasure of tallying up the register, its top spitting out an itemized receipt that I folded into quarters and slid into the deposit bag. My first pleasure in a profit not my own.

I took my other tasks more seriously, too. I turned my flashlight upon sneakers dangling across row tops, stopped a group of boys from throwing Raisinets at the screen, admonished talkers, confiscated a penlight, and even thwarted a would-be smoker, to the surprising applause of the theater audience. It was amazing what asserting myself could do. No longer did I read books by the corridor lights; I watched for feet, and kept an eye on couples passing a brown bag between them. I traded "Feet, please" for "Feet *off!*" and took my time walking the rows. If the crowd was small, I used the opportunity to roll the garbage to the dumpster, where I took care to sort the cardboard for recycling. I alerted Anton to the kids letting their friends in through the fire doors. I checked the screen for rips and tears.

But there were other changes, too. I talked to Alan more, and Janet, too. Janet lived with her mother, I learned, who was legally blind, but still liked to drive golf balls at the local driving range, where she was something of a celebrity. She and Janet would hit shots into the evening, until the range sweeper and the mosquitoes appeared, then go out for margaritas at Applebee's. Janet talked to me about college, too, which had always seemed exotic to me, since my parents never went, and since my ideas of college came from the movies, *Animal House* mostly. Janet told me how the dorms emptied out for the holidays, the campus like a beach town in the off-season. She told me about the library's notorious fourth floor, where the books were kept in tall cages, and where men were rumored to meet for sex. She told me about walking home from an evening class and seeing gray bats radiating out from the memorial bell tower. I told her about my bike ride home. She liked hearing about my game of closing my eyes. She laughed. It was the first time I had ever made a pretty girl laugh.

I talked to Alan about his kids, who were reading many of the same books I'd loved as a kid. *Incident at Hawk's Hill* and *From the Mixed-Up Files of Mrs. Basil E. Frankweiler.* Alan talked about his wife, who worked in a prison cafeteria and also drove a bus. She and Alan wanted to save enough money to buy a Winnebago and take the kids to Glacier National Park. He told me about his son, Alex, who could only fall asleep on the pullout bed in the living room, where the family dog, Flash, slept at his feet. Alan had another job working at a country club, but didn't want other people to know. Dishwashing, coat checking, banquet set-up. I began to see him as someone better, more qualified than the jobs he held, but unable to find suitable work. I didn't feel sorry for him since he didn't seem to feel sorry for himself. I liked that about him. I thought about Alan coming into the theater after an evening of checking people's coats at the country club. I began to imagine what life was like for someone totally different from myself. Sometimes I caught him dozing on the projection room stairs.

One evening was no one was around, I climbed onto the break room table and slid the ceiling tiles away. The pipe of drinking straws was still there, though dusty, and not as impressive as I'd remembered. I pulled it from its hiding place and folded it into a trash bag. Then I threw the bag into the dumpster, along with all of the evening's other garbage. I was about to relock the dumpster when I heard a faint crinkling noise and saw the pipe unfold itself from the bag, like a dead girl's finger in a horror movie. Its tip reached out and tapped me on the shoulder. I grabbed the pipe and, one by one, took apart every drinking straw. The straws were still in pretty good shape, despite the flattening on one end. Thick, sturdy straws. I got into it, taking them apart. I bundled them into a cardboard box, then sealed the box with packing tape and tossed it back into the dumpster.

That night I rode home. It was another beautiful summer night. Fat stars, a break in the humidity. I pedaled past houses with air conditioners turned off, windows open. From many of these, televisions glowed. Curtains divided my view from these rooms, but I discovered that I no longer imagined what was inside. I didn't even think about it. I coasted down Worley without even realizing I'd done so. Leaving the movies no longer held anything for me. I pushed my bicycle into the garage and lifted it onto a ceiling hook. The hook juddered against the sudden weight. The bike swayed, its rear tire spinning free. My thoughts got caught up in its motion. *Next time*, they said, *just take the car.*

<h1 style="text-align:center">FAMILY DEBATES,
1976–1983</h1>

I. Whether cousin Bobby really "ate" a sparkler during our Bicentennial picnic.

MOM: Until I pulled it out of his mouth, yes. But, no, he didn't *eat* it.

DAD: Don't remember.

SISTER: I remember him telling me he was going to do it, then hearing the rest from Uncle Oscar. Plus there's that picture of Bobby holding the sparkler, making a face like, *Mmm, delicious.* But the sparkler isn't even lit.

UNCLE OSCAR: All day he was telling me he was going to do it and then goddamned if he didn't just stick that thing right in. I was the one drove him to the emergency room. The doctors, or orderlies I guess, were dressed up like minute-men. Can you imagine that?

GRANDPOP: It was a pretzel, not a sparkler. He wouldn't stop running around with those sparklers, so I gave him a pretzel, you know, to keep him occupied. He made up the rest.

COUSIN BOBBY: I'll be spending Thanksgiving in Barbados, thanks.

II. Whether Dad faked a knee injury to avoid attending the Pope's visit to Philadelphia.

DAD: I've said it a thousand times: I had every intention of going with you, but tripped on one of those little wire fences, a wicket fence, I'd guess you call it, when we were all pushing through the crowd. I thought you saw it happen, but oh no, I've had to justify myself ever since. It's sad, when you think about it. Plus the knee still hurts sometimes when it rains.

MOM: Facts: A) There were no fences around. B) You'd complained all week about going, even saying, at one point, "What do I have to do, fake a knee injury?" C) You later admitted the whole thing in therapy.

SISTER: This one has always seemed a pretty easy call to me.

ME: I'm just glad I got to ride back with him. We stopped at Dairy Queen and had a few Dilly Bars until "the coast was clear."

III. Whose fault it was we wore matching I-Survived-the-Sooperdooperlooper! *T-shirts to Grandmom and Grandpop's surprise fiftieth anniversary party.*

MOM: I'm not talking about this again. I'm really not. But I will say this: did those T-shirts mean we don't *care* about Grandmom and Grandpop? Did those T-shirts *ruin* anyone's special memories or make the occasion any less special in any way?

DAD: It was your mother's fault.

SISTER: Mom.

ME: Mom.

GRANDMOM: I was able to nail polish—out the words in the group photo.

IV. Whether Dad's allergies were really the reason we couldn't keep Patches.

MOM: There were a variety of reasons, I'd guess you'd say, but yes, your father's allergies certainly topped the list. We've always made that clear.

DAD: I'm just glad I can cross the yard now. You know, without getting humped.

ME: He never seemed all that happy, really. Maybe he didn't like his name. Patches. Plus he was missing that eye.

MOM: That's *why* we named him Patches. We all agreed how cute that was.

DAD: I wanted "Clint Eastwood." There's a dog name you don't hear every day.

SISTER: I've never told you guys this before, but one time Patches tried to strangle me. It was right after we got back from Colonial Williamsburg. I thought he would have missed me, so I made up a little bed for him beside mine (Mom, this is also the true story behind the missing Christmas linens) but all Patches did was pee on it. I thought I'd clean things up, but Patches wouldn't get off the linens. I kept pulling at them, saying, "Patches, move! Bad doggie!" and the next thing I knew I was on my back and Patches was on top of me, sort of pinning my neck with the Christmas linens. He'd gotten them stuck between his paws, I guess.

MOM: Well, he's in a happier place now.

PATCHES: I know you're the ones who turned the squirrels against me.

V. What happened to the nativity set Uncle Randy made for us.

MOM: Ask your dad; he's the one who couldn't stop admiring it, remember? *Oh, let's put this under the tree right now. You've really outdone yourself this time, Randy.*

DAD: Well, if accepting gifts graciously is a crime, I'm guilty. Throw away the key.

SISTER: They were made out of beer bottles, right?

ME: Beer bottles and bottle-caps. He'd glued them together into little people.

DAD: Those weren't people; they were Jesus and Mary and Joseph.

MOM: Mary was St. Pauli Girl.

DAD: And Jesus was Budweiser—the King of Beers. It really was very creative, if you would have just given it a chance.

SISTER: The wise men smelled like cigars.

DAD: Their crowns were cigar rings.

SISTER: And their hands were made out of those fuzzy little wires.

ME: Pipe cleaners.

MOM: Those poked through the garbage bag.

VI. Was it a dog or a wolf that Dad swerved to avoid on our big drive out west?

MOM: Dog.

SISTER: Dog.

ME: I always thought this was just a story. You know, to explain hitting the guardrail.

SISTER: We were in Ohio. Who sees a wolf in Ohio?

MOM: Your father has never really been able to see at night, to tell the truth. One time we were driving home from the Olivers' house after a holiday party and your father kept saying he saw *coyotes*—on the Jersey Turnpike.

SISTER: Dad's always been weird about that stuff. Like the way he still Windexes the headlights before every big drive.

MOM: Or the way he calls everyone's high beams "bright eyes."

SISTER: Right. *Hey, take it easy there, bright eyes! Whoa, give us a break, bright eyes!*

DAD: Your mother reads your diary.

VII. The thing we never talk about.

ME: The thing we saw at the beach house, right?

SISTER: Right.

ME: I'm still not sure I saw it. But I guess I must have.

MOM: If it's anything you'd like to know about, your father and I are more than glad to talk about it. We've always thought you might ask about it someday. Or you can choose not to. We'll leave that up to you.

SISTER: We thought you were getting sick.

ME: The door was open.

SISTER: We walked right in.

ME: There were candles on the nightstand. And Mom in that—

SISTER: That's called "role playing," right?

DAD: You know what I remember most about that trip? The funny guitarist who sang us all those songs in that Mexican restaurant. Remember him? Boy, that guy loved to sing! I kept hoping he'd go away after a while, but no, he always had another song at the ready, you know? I bet he's still there today, singing his crazy songs. There was that one about the specials. That's the one I remember most. *Olé!*

VIII. What we'd do without these debates:

MOM: I don't know. Talk?

DAD: *Uno* Olympics!

SISTER: Learn about each other?

ME: Cry.

KIN, KIND

Twenty minutes before Act One, I have to drag Claudius outside for hurling a urinal puck at Laertes. We grapple inside the boys' bathroom, then make our way past the unlit trophy case and the orange-green lockers that give off a whiff of damp mittens and Fruit Roll-Ups. I've got him by the collar. He's got me by the cardigan. I am forty-four years old, and the theater director for the Pleasant Breeze School for Gifted Children. This year we're doing *Hamlet*.

"My dad's a lawyer," Claudius says.

We push through the fire doors and stand in the faculty parking lot. The lot is empty, except for a few cars and minivans with the flyers I designed pinched beneath their windshield wipers. Seeing them now, in the dim, purplish light, it occurs to me that I'd throw them away too.

"You bent my goddamn collar," Claudius says, even though I can see that this isn't true.

"That's a demerit," I say.

"Go to hell."

"That's two," I say, evenly, in the voice I developed for the "Gifted Kids, Gifted Teacher" seminar, the summer after the Pleasant Breeze Kindergarten *Die Walküre* disaster. Sometimes the voice reminds them. "Three, if you count the urinal thing," I say. I pause. Then, "You could be expelled."

Because it is cold, and because I'm sometimes good with the voice, and because Claudius is ten years old, he drops to the pavement and cries like a baby. "I hate you!" he wails, to the benefit of the parked cars and the school floodlights winking into life. "I hate you so *much!*"

Because it is good to let them cry sometimes, I allow Claudius to cry. Then I open the fire door again and brace my foot against its bottom.

"You have less than ten minutes to get your scepter and get yourself together," I say.

———

I'm the first to admit that the Pleasant Breeze Kindergarten *Die Walküre* was a complete embarrassment. I don't know why I insisted on it in the first place. Vanity? Probably so. Pride? Of course. I was new to the community back then, fresh, green. In love with the glow of my own flame. All that. When *Modern Gifted Educator* did a cover story on me, I had the article enlarged, dry-mounted, and tacked above my breakfast nook. How many times did I glance at the photos of me at the upright piano, one hand raised, marking the beat, as Wotan (Jimmy McKenzie) yanked a papier-mâché "fire" around Brunhilde (Nellie Sobocinski)?

Beneath the photo, a caption: *"This year they're doing*

Wagner," Owens says, with a charismatic smile. "*It's impossible for five-year-olds to do Wagner, but please don't tell them that. I don't want them to know.*"

—

Claudius doesn't return. So I go into my office and grab The Black Cloak that I keep on a special hook for occasions like these. I'm tying the ties that always give me such grief when Polonius walks in.

"Oh, don't tell me, Reginald," he says. "Don't. Tell. Me." He flops himself into the overstuffed bean bag chair I sometimes slept on during my marital separation, and throws his head back in disgust. When he speaks, the whatever inside the beanbag makes a crinkly noise.

"Don't you understand," he says, "why *no one* will accept you as an authority figure? Don't you understand that when you try to act otherwise, you end up ruining things for everyone? You do realize that, don't you?"

Because Polonius is four-foot-nine, his legs protrude from the beanbag like a grasshopper's antennae. I tell him that I've got things under control.

"Control? You call this control?" He tries to sit upright. "I call this *chaos!*"

His shouting summons Horatio and Fortinbras to my office door. They poke their heads in, sheepishly, until they catch sight of me in my cloak, loosening the adjustable band on the plastic crown that Claudius has left behind.

"Someone say this isn't happening," Horatio says.

"Oh, this is happening," Polonius says.

I place the crown upon my head.

"Someone say no," Fortinbras says.

Before anyone can say anything else, I swipe a safety pin from Horatio's cap and pin my cloak together. "Where's Hamlet?" I ask.

—

Before the lights dim, I step onto the stage and tap my fingers against the microphone that no one can ever figure out. I begin my usual speech. "Hello," I say, "and welcome." I tell the audience that it is my pleasure to see them here tonight. I tell the audience that I am humbled by their interest and enthusiasm for the theater.

"But mostly I want to say thanks," I say. "Thank you for letting me share the most precious gift I know." I smile. "Time with your gifted, gifted children."

—

I don't attempt to walk on my knees. I don't even bother stooping. Nor do I show surprise when the audience gasps as I walk onstage, and lob my lines over the heads of Gertrude and Polonius. I finish my speech and take my wobbly throne with all the dignity and aplomb of an elephant settling into a thimble.

"*And now, Laertes,*" Laertes whispers, cueing me, as I see Hamlet across the stage, catching his eye for the first time. In it, I glimpse a slick disappointment.

When I say, "*But now, my cousin Hamlet, and my son—*" the audience titters. Hamlet passes before me, in a way that violates the blocking diagram we revised together at Denny's, then speaks his first line. His voice is a brushed drum.

"*A little more than kin, and less than kind.*"

From the back rows I hear whispers.

Because Gertrude is the only one who didn't goof off at my Method Acting/Kiwanis Kanoe Kamp Retreat, she now turns on me a perfect "Extreme Disgust" facial contortion, then begins her speech.

By the time I finish my closing lines, the audience has twice been shushed by the Ghost of Hamlet's Father, who sits at the back of auditorium working the lights and worrying the icing off the vanilla nut cupcakes no one will want by intermission. The audience whispers because I am a forty-four-year-old man dressed in a black cape and plastic crown, struggling to

liberate myself from a desk-chair throne. Because Hamlet has
to help wrestle it from my backside.

Because I am Claudius, and Hamlet is my son.

—

During the third scene, I spot Hamlet in the backstage
lounge, scribbling a Worry Note with the thin black marker
I've tied to the Worry Tree. I stand next to him, and tell him
I'm sorry. But he only takes a Worry Pin and fastens the note
to the tree.

I'M WORRIED THAT: *you don't care about humiliating
me.*

I take the marker and fasten a note to a different Worry
Branch, tossing aside the note that reads I'M WORRIED THAT:
the Worry Tree is rotting my precocious mind!

I'M WORRIED THAT: *you won't forgive me.*

Hamlet sighs, taking the marker.

I'M WORRIED THAT: *why is everything always about
you?*

I'M WORRIED THAT: *sorry sorry. You know I've been trying to work on that lately.*

I'M WORRIED THAT: *Mom says you've been saying that
forever.*

I'M WORRIED THAT: *yes, I know, I know.*

I'M WORRIED THAT: *if you know so much, why doesn't
it seem like it?*

I'M WORRIED THAT: *I've spent many a sleepless night
wondering that myself.*

I'M WORRIED THAT: *sad.*

I'M WORRIED THAT: *help me, son.*

Hamlet looks at me, and I can tell he's thinking of putting
a hand to my shoulder, the way he used to when we practiced
our bagpipe and Theremin sonatas together, the music filling
the nursery while his mother worked the camcorder. I consider
reminding him, but end up capping the marker instead. Since
it is his way to hesitate, he hesitates now, looking away. Then

he whispers, "I'm on," and passes through the heavy curtain his mother and I once used as a bedsheet during a particularly ardent reprieve in our sad and mystifying marriage.

—

But who can explain the end of marriage? Would it help to overhear us, on a wooded path, taking a family walk? Would it help to feel the silences between us, heavy as damp towels, as our son romped in the leaves, saying *Look, Mom, Dad, look.* Do you want him to bring a salamander to us, plucked from the underside of a rotted log? Do you want him to cup it between his palms, saying *He's tickling me, Dad, ha!* Do you want him to place it in my hands, me crouching, saying *He's something, isn't he?* my knee damp and cold in the soggy path? Do you want my son to ask, *But Dad, why are you crying?* as a couple on bicycles slows to pass, senses our misery, then speeds away?

Do you?

—

My son is gentle with the foil. For this I am thankful.

I hook my thumb around one arm of the throne, then push it away, falling to a heap at the boots we both agreed looked better with the Timberland logo inked out.

O, yet defend me, friends, I am but hurt.

I roll to one side and die with my eyes open. From here, I can see everything: the empty seats with programs tented across the arms, Horatio's fat parents in the middle rows, studying me like I'm a museum display, Ophelia's mother, front row, center, wondering, I'm sure, if I've gotten around to reading her autobiographical play—*The Gingerbread Girl, Crumbling*—she unloaded at our last parent-teacher meeting, and Fortinbras and the Ambassadors tittering in the wings, exchanging the purple Game Boy I confiscated last semester, whose giddy lights and cheery beeps eased me through so many turbulent nights.

Hamlet falls beside me and dies. I hear his breath subside, and hope he's remembered the death meditation we rehearsed over pizza and Whack-A-Mole: *A beautiful garden, fenced by sunflowers. I find stairs to the garden and descend. At the base, another stairway, smaller and covered with moss.* I'm pleased to see that he keeps his eyes open, a touch of naturalism I recommended, his fingers twitching, lightly. Because Hamlet has angled himself slightly away from downstage, our eyes meet. I see the expert nothingness there, and want to tell him I'm proud. We lie that way, dead, father and son, suppressing blinks, twitches.

It occurs to me that we haven't had time together like this in the longest while.

—

On the drive home, we do not speak. It is raining, and I'm thankful for the how-do?-how-do? of the wipers. Our bodies exude the smell of Noxzema and hair rinse. Miles later, my son's voice.

"Dad," he says, "I think I'm done with things for a while." He does not look over. "I mean, plays and stuff."

"I see." We pull into the neighborhood entranceway.

"I don't know," he says, "I just don't think I'm into it anymore."

"Into it," I say.

We turn onto our street—*his* street—and I see our house—*his* house—with the porch light on. His mother's Acura is in the drive, a car I've never known.

"Swear you won't be mad," he says.

I stop the car at the curb, listening to the rain, engine.

"Swear it."

I look over and see the black around his ears, the spots where the hairspray strayed. There are crusts of cold cream in his eyebrows.

"I swear," I say.

He hugs me good-bye, then takes off into the rain, running across the lawn. I watch him fumble for his key, then wave, before the door opens and the house swallows him whole. And then I spot his book bag behind the passenger's seat, forgotten. I grab it and open my door.

I feel rain in my hair. I see the front door. Because the lawn is wet and muddy, I hop the flagstone walkway, and hear water splattering beneath me. Because I am a foolish man, carrying a red book bag in the rain, I allow myself this one small pleasure: I see myself as I wish my son might, a father at the door, knocking.

THE ISLAND

When Graham's bus stopped at Fox Crossing, he did something that surprised himself: he stood and grabbed his book bag. Fox Crossing wasn't his stop—he lived on Tangier Drive—but he followed Kevin Reynolds to the front of the bus as the driver pulled the door open with a wide, paddling motion, and felt as if he were about to parachute from a tremendous height.

"This isn't your stop," the driver said.

"I know."

The driver sighed and glanced out the side-view mirror, where the flashing lights of another bus could be seen like a dumb, insistent bug. Graham watched as a tiny hand emerged from the driver's window of the bug-bus, and waved. "Waves," the driver said, then laughed. "*Waves* at me."

Graham stepped off the bus and stood next to Kevin.

"I can only drive them," the driver said, apparently to no one. "That's all I can do." He pulled the door shut and, for a moment, it was as if the bus had spoken, then closed its mouth, but Graham knew this was ridiculous. He put his book bag over his shoulder and watched the bus shudder down the lane. It was the last day of school and the air was thick with honeysuckle.

—

For years, an ornamental bench had stood alongside the FOX CROSSING entrance sign, the centerpiece of a raised, landscaped island that divided the main drive into two separate thoroughfares. At night a floodlight shone upon the sign, casting the bench into shadows and, on the few evenings when Graham had chanced to pass by, he had imagined the two involved in a kind of dialogue, a vague, mysterious conversation that subsided every time a car passed by. The idea fascinated him.

Now Graham climbed up onto the island—this was higher than he had imagined it, somehow—and stood next to the bench, feeling, for the first time that day, a sense of ease. Sitting down, he was surprised to discover that the bench wasn't nearly as fragile as he had imagined. He ran his hand along its arms, smooth and sun-warmed, like his own, and felt the solidity of the legs beneath, cooler, hidden from the sun. Behind him, four young saplings, each tied to wooden stakes, offered an envelope of shade. Graham leaned back and waited for a car to pass.

When the wind picked up, the saplings tugged against their ropes.

—

The day had begun with Graham helping his mother's boyfriend to bed. Dale worked nights, and, not wanting to wake Graham's mother, occasionally camped out on the family room sofa, a thin blanket drawn to his chin, a nearly-finished bowl of cereal on the coffee table before him. This morning, Graham had taken the bowl into the kitchen and rinsed it, hoping the sound of running water would wake Dale, but it did nothing. Dale was sleeping with his head propped on the armrest, shoulders hunched, tightly, as if cradling a phone receiver.

Graham stood before him and whispered his name. "Dale," he said. "It's morning."

Outside, the sun was just coming up. The room was not yet warm. Graham whispered his name again, observing now a change in Dale's expression. Gone were the tight shoulders and arms drawn to his chest. His mouth parted, as if anticipating a kiss. There was a tenderness in these changes that was confusing to Graham, as the Dale he did not know offered a glimpse of the Dale he wished he loved. "Dale," he said. "It's time."

Dale sat up.

"Time to get up and go to bed."

Dale rubbed his eyes. "Story of my life," he said.

Upstairs, Graham heard Dale open the bedroom door. He wondered if his mother had overslept her alarm again. He listened for sounds of conversation, heard none, then climbed to the top of the stairs. The bedroom door was open. He moved to the doorway, taking in a view of his mother, asleep, her body angled diagonally across the bed. Dale slept atop the covers in the slight space afforded to him. Graham knew he would have to wake his mother—she counted on him as her second alarm—but, for now, he sat on the edge of the bed and listened to her breathing, the three of them together, like a family, breathing, sleeping.

Dreaming.

———

Graham opened his book bag, looking for anything to pass the time. Inside, he found a five-subject notebook, two glossy folders, and a social studies workbook he'd forgotten to hand in. He put the workbook aside and opened the smaller pocket, hunting for a pen. It felt strange to look for a pen and think of the bus heading towards his road, no longer needing to stop.

He was about to open the workbook when he heard the sound of a school bus approaching. The bus slowed to a stop, one sleepy-looking boy staring out at Graham from the front row, regarding him as disappointedly as if he were a dropped penny. The bus door opened; two girls stepped down to the pavement. When the second girl reached the ground, she cupped her hands to her mouth and yelled, "Eeez diz dee French pol*ice*?" to which the first girl dropped her book bag and broke down laughing.

As the bus rolled away, a back window clicked open, and another voice cried out, "Ja, diz eez dee French pol*ice*!" and the two girls hugged their arms to their chests and laughed.

"I can't believe it!" the first girl said.

"What can't you believe, Mademoiselle? Dat sheez dee French pol*ice*?"

The first girl dropped to her knees.

"Don't chu be-lieve in dee French pol*ice*?"

Graham realized that the girls did not see him, and spoke as if they were alone. He felt embarrassed to think that they might notice him on the bench, with his book bag on his lap, watching them. These were older girls, too, junior high. He considered making an obvious noise, when the first girl performed a little spin and spotted him.

"Oh," she said, and the second girl turned to follow her gaze. Graham sensed that waving was somehow out of the question, and pulled his lips together in a grim, acknowledging smile.

"A boy on dee bench," the second girl said. The two girls looked at each other, expecting, Graham thought, to laugh again, but he was disappointed when they only continued on their way. As they passed behind him, Graham heard the first girl say, "He shouldn't be up there. That's not a sitting bench," and those words were like a hand upon his shoulder. He listened as their voices grew smaller and smaller, returning him to the sound of his own breathing. A yellow car passed by, and Graham tried to make out the face of the driver.

———

Rush hour, Graham discovered, did not begin around five, as he had previously imagined; it began at four. He sat with the workbook opened across his lap, beginning a chapter that hadn't been assigned, as cars entered the neighborhood, a few slowing when they spotted him, then moving along. Graham was happy when a pick-up honked its blatty horn, but saddened to see it speed away like the others. He returned to his work, the feeling of answering the unassigned questions like finding an unseen banister in a darkened stairwell.

The chapter should have been the day's lesson in social studies, but Mr. Rivers had surprised the class with a last-day party, and the lesson had been ignored. When Graham entered the classroom, he found the ceiling webbed with streamers, the desks arranged in a circle, and a side table fitted out with cake, chips, and bottles of soda. He looked to Mr. Rivers for some kind of explanation, but the Mr. Rivers he knew, the one who addressed them by surname, the one who shook his wristwatch in the middle of class, glancing up at the clock with clear dissatisfaction, had been replaced by a happier, jokier Mr. Rivers, only too glad to serve a slice of cake or refill an empty cup.

After his classmates had departed, Graham helped straighten up the room. He collected paper plates and half-finished drinks, as Mr. Rivers pushed the desks back into rows. "I'd think you'd be happy to get a head start on your summer," he said, giving Graham a smile. "But I appreciate the help."

Graham nodded, then went to the opposite side of the room and pushed a desk back into place. The metal undersides were cool to his hands, and its empty interior rumbled like a drummed tin.

"Oh, you don't have to do that," Mr. Rivers said.

"It's OK," Graham said. "I can stay."

Mr. Rivers laughed. "Well, if I had known I'd get such student devotion, I would have had a party a long time ago," he said, and Graham felt a tightening in his throat. When they finished, Graham grabbed his book bag and paused in the doorway, regarding the neat, uniform rows of desks as Mr. Rivers closed the classroom windows; windows that looked out upon a row of curbside buses, their engines idling.

—

Across the street was an undeveloped lot, a sloping field of high grass, and low, umbrella-shaped apple trees. A wire fence separated the road from the field, and all afternoon Graham could see insects drifting above the grass, passing through the fence as if it were a shadow. He was just finishing the assignment when a white station wagon passed before him, then slowed to a stop in the narrow strip of grass between road and fence. He put his pen in his book and closed the cover.

Through the driver's side window, Graham saw an elderly woman, her head so low to the dash that it looked as if she were sleeping, her husband sitting beside her. The husband opened his door and moved to the back of the car, his walk slow and disjointed, as if he'd just traded ice skates for loafers, and waited as another car drove by. When the car passed, he opened the back hatch and removed an empty laundry basket—the plastic kind Graham's mother used—and set it on the ground. His shirt was torn in places.

The man carried the basket to the fence, crouched down, and began filling it with fallen apples. He started by throwing them in one at a time, stopping to inspect quality, but the woman yelled something out the window and he began tossing them in two at a time, three at a time. The basket began to fill. When another car drove by, the man continued his work, sticking his arms into the high grass and tossing apples into the basket. He did not look up.

Graham watched as another car passed, saddened to see the driver ignore the couple, then realized, suddenly, that the woman was watching him. He put his chin to his chest, hoping she would look away, but when he raised his head, she was still there, watching. There were clips in her hair, black ones. She turned and said something to her husband, as he carried the basket to the rear and placed it inside the car. He closed the door, then regarded Graham, momentarily, as he wiped his hand across his forehead. When the car rolled away, Graham saw him straightening his hat.

Graham stood up and hopped down from the island. He had not noticed, until now, that his clothes stuck to his back, and that his legs were cramped from sitting. He crossed the street, feeling as if he were waking from a long, restless sleep. He thought of Dale. He thought of him sleeping through the day, the shades pulled tight, his body draped across the covers. He thought of him waking, wandering through the house with robe straps untied, his feet bare. He thought of him finding a blanket neatly folded atop the family room sofa.

There were tread marks in the grass from where the station wagon had been. Graham stood where the husband had, and knelt into the grass. Underneath, he found the ground beaded with red-brown apples, their skins as pocked and mottled as a whale's belly. He plucked one from the ground, and found its underside rotten and wet. He tossed it aside and selected another, this one lighter, firmer, and placed it inside his book bag. His hands grew damp. A book bag was perfect for gathering apples. Graham had no idea. He filled every pocket, every pouch.

On the way back to the island he tossed two apples at a fire hydrant.

—

When it had just begun to get dark outside, the spotlight clicked on. This was brighter than Graham had imagined. A feeling like being onstage. Graham moved to the other side of the bench, but this did no good. If he put his legs up, a shadow fell across his face. This would have to do. He watched a few more cars pass. If his mother was awake when he got home, he would ask her to make him a grilled cheese. Sometimes that made things better, when she made a grilled cheese. "So," she would say, setting the plate before him. But Graham wouldn't say anything. He'd dip the sandwich in ketchup as his father had liked to do.

A few moments later, a maroon Cutlass slowed into the entranceway. The sound of its engine was as familiar to Graham as the sight of its long, banded grille and round headlights. He sat up and gathered his things together. Dale pulled the car to the curb. When Graham got to the door Dale leaned over to unlock it for him. There was a bag of fast food on the passenger's seat. Graham set it atop his lap and fastened his seatbelt.

"A neighbor called," Dale explained. He did not elaborate.

They drove a while, not speaking. Graham nibbled on a cheeseburger, watching neighborhoods passing in the distance. Looking over, he saw that Dale wore jeans and bedroom slippers, his pale ankles poking out as he moved from gas to brake. His collar was bent upward, and, when he turned to check an intersection, Graham saw that the shirt was on backwards, the tag sticking out. He wiped his mouth, and remembered Dale sleeping on the sofa, waking with eyes still closed.

"You must really hate me sometimes," Dale said. He did not look over.

"No," Graham whispered, but his head was down, and he knew that Dale could not hear.

"It's too much," Dale said. "Too much for a kid."

They turned onto Tangier Drive, and Graham saw his house in the distance. Upstairs, the bedroom shades were still drawn, but below, the garage door was open, the inside light left on. As they approached, Graham could see the day's paper still in the drive, its middle blown across the walk.

"Too much for anyone," Dale said.

"No," Graham whispered. He felt Dale looking at him, and, for a moment it was like sitting on the bed, the day not yet begun. Graham reached over and touched the sleeve of Dale's shirt.

"I was so afraid," he said. "I was so afraid no one would come."

ACKNOWLEDGMENTS

The author would like to thank the editors of the magazines in which some of these stories first appeared: *Boulevard* ("The Walkers"); *Charleston Post and Courier* ("Kin, Kind"); *Epoch* ("In the Age of Automobiles"); *Fugue* ("Family Debates, 1976–1983"); *Gettysburg Review* ("The Girl at the Station"); *Greensboro Review* ("The Fall of Rome"); *Harvard Review* ("Toro"); *Indiana Review* ("The French Girls"); *Mid-American Review* ("The Summer He Was Seven"); *New England Review* ("Parade Rest"); *Other Voices* ("Out Loud"); *Shenandoah* ("The Island," under the title "Daylight Savings"); *South Carolina Review* ("Like That," under the title "Places of Comfort").

"The Summer He Was Seven" was selected by Michael Martone as winner of an AWP Intro Journals Award.

"Kin, Kind" was selected by Maud Casey and Murad Kalam as a winner of the South Carolina Fiction Project.

I would also like to thank the National Endowment for the Arts for their support, as well as my teachers, colleagues, and students at the University of Missouri-Columbia and the College of Charleston. A special thanks to Scott Turow and the University of Pittsburgh Press for all their editorial wisdom and guidance.

I am immensely thankful for my friends and family; their

enthusiasm helped carry me along. And, finally, I would like to thank my wife, Malinda, my first reader, whose writing continues to amaze me; my son, Gus, for always asking for one more book, and my daughter, Ruby, for listening to me read out loud.